GROOVES

GROOVES

A KIND OF MYSTERY

Kevin Brockmeier

KATHERINE TEGEN BOOKS

An Imprint of HarperCollins*Publishers*

Grooves: A Kind of Mystery

Copyright © 2006 by Kevin Brockmeier

For information address HarperCollins Children's Books, a division of HarperCollins Publishers, 1350 Avenue of the Americas, New York, NY 10019.

www.harperchildrens.com

Library of Congress Cataloging-in-Publication Data
Brockmeier, Kevin.
   Grooves : a kind of mystery / Kevin Brockmeier.—1st ed.
      p.   cm.
   Summary: After a seventh grader discovers that the grooves in his Thigpen-brand blue jeans are encoded with a cry for help, he sets out to save the factory workers from greedy entrepreneur Howard Thigpen.
   ISBN-10: 0-06-073691-7
   ISBN-10: 0-06-073692-5 (lib. bdg.)
   ISBN-13: 978-0-06-073691-0
   ISBN-13: 978-0-06-073692-7 (lib. bdg.)
   [1. Jeans (Clothing)—Fiction.   2. Factories—Fiction. 3. Mystery and detective stories.]   I. Title.
PZ7.B7828G7 2006   2004022683
[Fic]—dc22   CIP
                                                                      AC

Typography by Hilary Zarycky
1 2 3 4 5 6 7 8 9 10
❖
First Edition

For Eric Carter,
in honor of our many adventures

ONE

My favorite teacher at Howard Thigpen Junior High School is Mr. Fred. Mr. Fred wins the contest hands down. His official teacher name is Fred Boosey—that's what it says beside his picture in the yearbook—but he's the sort of teacher who allows the kids to call him by his first name.

One of the things I like so much about Mr. Fred is that you never know from one day to the next which teacher you're going to get: the normal one or the complete loon. For instance, last Christmas the student council decorated all the classrooms with these creepy-looking plastic elf statues. Instead of flowing white beards they all had dark stubble on their faces. They looked like the world's smallest escaped convicts. Mr. Fred lined them up on the floor and threw chalkboard erasers at them. He called it "Bowling for Elves."

And then there was the day he phoned in sick,

but came to class early and hid inside the podium. Mr. Fred is a little guy, shaped something like half of a hot dog—the kind of person who can easily fit inside a podium. As the substitute teacher read our lesson to us, Mr. Fred began wheeling the podium across the floor behind her back. Every time she turned around, it would be a few inches farther away. Finally she figured out that something was going on, and when she stood up and reached for the podium, Mr. Fred rolled himself right out the door. He made her chase him down the hallway. It cracked everybody up!

I figure Mr. Fred must be bored teaching physical science to a bunch of zoned-out seventh graders all the time—otherwise why would he do so many crazy things? But even the kids who normally just fall asleep on their desks in other classes always stay wide awake during his. He's got this talent.

The other thing I like so much about Mr. Fred is that he almost never spends the entire hour just reading to us from the textbook. Instead, he likes to help us conduct science experiments, real ones, making Möbius strips and mixing chemicals and things like that.

The week I want to tell you about, the most exciting week of my life, began the day Mr. Fred taught us about record players and how they amplify sound.

It was a Monday morning, and he started class by taking roll through a cardboard loudspeaker, the kind that cheerleaders use when they want to badger the fans at a game into roaring and clapping and behaving like a bunch of yahoos and rowdies, which is what my grandfather always calls them. By the time Mr. Fred came to the three Bobbies in a row—Bobby Piccolo, Bobby Ray, and Bobby Roberts—the entire room had gone quiet. We were all trying to figure out what he was up to.

"DWAYNE RUGGLES?" he said through the loudspeaker.

I answered, "Here."

That's my name, Dwayne Ruggles. There's a group of eighth graders who like to wobble their bellies and say "ruggles, ruggles, ruggles" every time they see me. They do this, and then they fall over laughing. They sound like the Hamburglar from the McDonald's TV commercials. I can never figure it out.

I admit that Dwayne Ruggles isn't the best name in the world, but I can live with it.

"And that's everybody," Mr. Fred said, shutting his roll book. "All right. Today, folks, we're going to conduct an experiment in sound." He brought the bullhorn back to his lips. "THUS THE LOUD-SPEAKER." He put it back down.

"Now why does my voice seem so much bigger when I speak through the loudspeaker? It's because it concentrates the sound waves I produce—it squeezes them together—and this makes them louder." He drew a picture on the board to illustrate. "If you're standing outside and you want to call to your friends, but you think they won't be able to hear you, what do you do? You cup your hands around your mouth. Well, a loudspeaker works the same way."

Mr. Fred handed everybody a sheet of construction paper, a few strips of tape, and a straight pin. He told us to roll the paper into a cone and tape it shut so that it looked like the loudspeaker. "Then I want you to puncture the smaller opening with the straight pin. Just push it all the way through. Like so," he said, and he pressed the straight pin through the construction paper so that it split the hole right in two.

After we had all finished making our cones, he gave us each a pencil and a record album. Most kids don't own record albums nowadays, but everybody has at least seen one before, if not at home then in music videos or in dance clubs, where dj's use them to make that *whick-a whick-a whick-a* sound.

"Now," Mr. Fred explained, "with a record album, the music is locked inside the grooves in the form of tiny swerves and ripples. If you spin the record around, the pin will follow those swerves and ripples and pick up the sound, which will pass through the needle into the cone. And what will the cone do? It will make the music louder so you can hear it."

He told us to stick the pencil through the hole in the center of the record, spin it like a top, and then hold the needle to the groove. I tried to do this, but the lead on my pencil was broken, and my record just kept toppling over and whirling into my chest. Mr. Fred leaned over and whispered some advice into my ear. "Try using the eraser end,

Dwayne. It will spin a lot better that way."

It worked just like he said it would. I could feel the construction paper vibrating in my hand as the needle traced the grooves in the record, around and around and around. Music came streaming out of the wide end of the cone. Every time I gave the pencil another twirl, the singer's voice would go really fast for a while, then it would sound normal for a few seconds, and then gradually it would slow down, so that half the time he sounded like a chipmunk and half the time he sounded like a drugged-out hippie. This is something else my grandfather likes to call people. It was pretty neat.

It turned out that Mr. Fred had given everybody the exact same record—"Ghostbusters" by Ray Parker Jr. I didn't know the song, but I could hear the lyrics coming from every single desk in the room.

"Who you gonna call? Ghostbusters!"

"If you've had a dose of a freaky ghost, baby, you'd better call Ghostbusters!"

"Let me tell you somethin'—Bustin' makes me feel good!"

It reminded me of the song "Monster Mash," if

you've ever heard that one before, only it made a lot less sense.

One of the girls who sat behind me raised her hand and asked Mr. Fred, "Why do you have so many copies of 'Ghostbusters' by Ray Parker Jr.?"

Mr. Fred rolled his eyes. He said that he had won fifteen thousand copies of "Ghostbusters" on a game show when he was in college. They were stacked all over his house now—in his bedroom, in his kitchen, everywhere. Sometimes, on clear summer days, he used them as frisbees. "Let me give you a piece of advice, kids. If you're ever on *Let's Make a Deal* and you have a choice between a brand-new kitchen set or what's behind Door Number One, always stick with the brand-new kitchen set."

I was having a really good time with my record album and my makeshift loudspeaker. I found that with a little practice I could control the spinning so that the music sounded almost normal, or at least as normal as "Ghostbusters" was likely to sound. Every so often I would bump the record with my thumb and it would come rattling to a stop, but I thought I was doing pretty good for a beginner.

I decided that I would look through some of my grandfather's old record albums when I got home and see if I could continue the experiment there.

Just before the hour ended, Principal McNutt came over the intercom to remind us that instead of going to our next class, we were supposed to report to the auditorium during second period to listen to a special guest speaker. We have special guest speakers about once a month at Howard Thigpen Junior High School. Usually they talk to us about one of two things: the dangers of smoking and peer pressure or why it's important to go to college. I can't say that I've ever had any interest in smoking, and I do want to go to college, but there's only so many times you can hear all this before your mind starts to drift and you daydream about dropping out of school with your friends and smoking cigarettes left and right. The best guest speaker we ever had was the ex-astronaut who told us what it was like to live on a space station for six months. He said that it was difficult to eat cookies in space because the crumbs would float all over the place, but it was fun to play marbles there for the same reason.

The bell rang, and Mr. Fred said, "Don't forget the Science Fair is coming up next month, folks. I want to see your proposals by this time next week."

We all poured out of the classroom and headed for the assembly.

And that was where the mystery started and things began to get really weird.

TWO

After I dropped my books off at my locker, I went to the auditorium to find my best friend, Kevin Applebab. Kevin Applebab and I have been best friends ever since the second grade, when he moved here to North Mellwood with his mom and dad. Kevin is a lot taller than I am, so it was pretty easy for me to spot him. A few summers ago he had a growth spurt while he was staying with his uncle in Chicago. When he came back to town, he was more than six feet tall and skinny as a stick. Before then he had been only four-and-a-half feet tall and shaped like a turnip or Danny DeVito—like I am.

The same summer Kevin had his growth spurt, he started wearing glasses. He wears the type that are supposed to darken into sunglasses whenever you go outside and turn back into regular glasses as soon as you come back in, but I've noticed that glasses like these never seem to work right. Kevin Applebab's are always a muddy shade of brown no matter where he happens to be.

Kevin was sitting in the third row of the auditorium, and he waved to me as soon as I walked through the door. After I sat down, I asked him if he had figured out what he was going to do for his science fair project yet. "Well, I'm thinking of doing something with my hamsters," he said. "But I don't know for sure."

"Neither do I. We have to come up with something by next Monday, though. That's what Mr. Fred said."

Kevin Applebab also had Mr. Fred for physical science, but not until the seventh period. The way I figured it, I was lucky to begin my day with Mr. Fred, but Kevin Applebab was even luckier to end his day with him. "Hamsters it is, then," he said. "Maybe I'll send them through a maze or something."

"You should blindfold them first. Or spin them around to make them dizzy. Something to make the whole thing more challenging."

The lights fell in the auditorium. It turned out

that our guest speaker was Howard Thigpen—the same Howard Thigpen our school is named after. Our school used to be called William Henry Harrison Junior High School, after the ninth president of the United States, but then Howard Thigpen donated something like a million dollars for us to build a football field, and the town council voted to change the name. The whole thing made me feel kind of bad for William Henry Harrison. I mean, from what I could tell he was a pretty useless president—he caught pneumonia at his inauguration and died a month later—but he never did any real harm. I hated to see him tossed aside just because he never bought anybody a football field.

Howard Thigpen did not talk about peer pressure or the dangers of smoking. He did not talk about the importance of going to college. Instead, he talked about what it was like to be rich, and why being rich was such a good thing to be.

"It's only when you have enough money," he said, "that you can behave as though money doesn't matter. For instance, if you children are in the grocery store with your parents and you want to buy a candy bar, you have to ask your parents for the money—and they may or may not give it to you. On the other hand, your parents can buy themselves all the candy bars they want, and they can do it without asking a solitary soul. Why? Because they have enough money.

"Well, I have more money than all of your parents combined," he said. "The whole world is my candy bar. If I want a car, I buy it. If I want a house, I buy it. If I want a school, I buy it. When I first came to North Mellwood, I had only enough money to open one blue jeans factory. Now, five years later, I own seven different factories manufacturing seven different products. Thigpen Brand Potato Chips. Thigpen Brand Tennis Shoes. Thigpen Brand Toothbrushes. Thigpen Brand Pigpens. Thigpen Brand Shaving Cream.

"How did I accomplish all this, you ask? Money. I thought about it and thought about it and thought about it—how to make it, how to invest it, how to spend it. And now that I have it, I don't have to think about it anymore. I pay people to think about it for me. What I have discovered, children, is that you can pay people to do anything you want. *Anything*.

"A demonstration," he said, and he pointed to a kid sitting in the front row. "You—Curly. Come here for a moment."

The kid Howard Thigpen had pointed to made his way to the microphone. I recognized him from my neighborhood. He was a ninth grader with curly red hair and a sea of freckles on his face—who was, in fact, generally known as Curly. Howard Thigpen pulled out his wallet and said, "I'll give you fifty dollars to squawk like a chicken."

"Are you serious?" Curly asked.

"Quite serious," said Howard Thigpen.

Without even thinking, the kid went, "*Buk-buk-buk-bukawh!*" and flapped his elbows a little. He even let his head go loose on his neck, jabbing it in and out like a chicken would. It was a pretty impressive performance. I could have done a better job myself, but then my chicken imitation is my specialty. People tell me they can't tell it apart from the real thing.

Howard Thigpen gave Curly a fifty-dollar bill, and then he pointed into the audience again and said, "You—girl. Come join us."

A girl I had never noticed before took the stage. She had dark brown hair and dark brown eyes, and she wore a green army jacket. She reminded me a little of Cinnamon Holmes, the girl who used to babysit for me when I was in elementary school. It kind of made me feel like I knew her.

"I'll give you fifty dollars to pretend that you're spinning a hula hoop," Howard Thigpen told the girl.

Fifty dollars is a lot of money. I was sure that most of the kids in the audience—myself included—would have been happy to squawk like a chicken or pretend they were spinning a hula hoop or even both at the same time for fifty dollars. But the girl just stared at him and furrowed her brow. For a minute I didn't think she was going to do it. Finally, though, she shrugged her shoulders and said, "Why not?"

I don't know if you've ever seen a person pretending to hula hoop without an actual hula hoop before, but it looks pretty funny. She began rolling her waist in a giant circle. Her arms went seesawing up and down and her stomach kept ballooning forward and then collapsing in on itself. She looked like she was having some sort of fit. The whole audience practically fell over laughing. When she was finished, Howard Thigpen gave her a fifty-dollar bill.

"As I said," Howard Thigpen told us, "you can pay people to do anything you want. But perhaps you children still don't believe me, so I will offer one more demonstration." He asked Principal McNutt to join him at the microphone, and the principal came clacking onto the stage in his hard leather shoes. His scalp shone bright red through a few thin wisps of white hair. This is what happened to him whenever he became angry.

"What's the meaning of all this?" the principal rumbled. "We didn't invite you here today just so you could toss your money around and force the children to make chicken noises. Don't you have anything at all to say about peer pressure or cigarettes or the importance of going to college?"

"I'll give you fifty dollars," Howard Thigpen answered, "to stand on one foot and sing 'I'm a Pretty Little Buttercup.'"

"I don't know 'I'm a Pretty Little Buttercup.' And anyway—"

"Any song you want to, then," Howard Thigpen said.

"Absolutely not."

"A hundred dollars."

"I'll never do it."

Howard Thigpen grinned and said, "Your principal is a man of . . . principle, children. But nobody is without his price." He leaned over and whispered something into Principal McNutt's ear.

Principal McNutt looked uncomfortable for a few seconds, like a man who has swallowed a rotten peanut. I swallowed a rotten peanut myself once, so I know what I'm talking about. Then he frowned and stood on one foot and sang, "*Girls, they want to have fun! Oh, girls just want to have fun! When the working day is done, girls—they want to have fun! Oh, girls just want to have fun!*" This went on for a good three minutes. I could hear the kids around me tittering and singing along with him under their breath. He was using a surprisingly little-girlish falsetto, and so were they. I knew that I would be hearing Principal McNutt impressions for the rest of the week, if not the year.

Howard Thigpen had been writing a check out as he listened, and he tore it loose from his checkbook and handed it to Principal McNutt. "You can take your seat now," he said. The principal stopped singing and headed bashfully down the stairs, followed by the boy who had squawked like a chicken and the girl who had spun an imaginary hula hoop.

"There you have it," Howard Thigpen said, opening his arms wide. "Behold the power of money."

He looked so pleased with himself that he was almost glowing. It was only when I looked closer that I realized he actually *was* glowing.

Or sort of.

At first I thought it was just the glare from the spotlights bouncing off the stage, but where his shadow should have been—beneath his chin and under his arms and at his feet—I could see sparks of light swirling and jumping. They looked kind of like the spots you see when you stand up too quickly and the blood rushes to your head, except that they didn't go away. Whenever he moved, no matter how slightly, they shifted to fill the new shadows. I closed my eyes and looked again, but they were still there.

"Money, children, is the most important thing in the world," Howard Thigpen said. "You should do everything you can to get it and to keep it. That's the first rule of business, which is the first rule of life, and I pass it on to you today. With enough money, you can make anyone, anyone at all, your own personal candy bar.

"And for a truly mouthwatering candy bar," he finished, "try Thigpen Brand Angel Bars—the bar with that heavenly crunch."

THREE

I was still thinking about Howard Thigpen and the lights inside his shadow when I got home from school that afternoon. I live with my grandfather over Oliver's Antique Store. That's my grandfather's name, Oliver. He has operated his antique store for more than forty-seven years, and every June, on his birthday, he repaints the sign above the front door: OPEN (AND CLOSED ON WEDNESDAY) FOR <u>47</u> YEARS. The store is the kind of place where you can barely even open the door without knocking over a wicker table or a lamp or something. Everything is stuffed into one big room, and eight or nine tiny paths wind their way from one antique pile to another. Most of the antiques are just junk, really—old *TV Guide*s, enormous springs with seat cushions attached to them, faded tin signs, things like that. If you look hard enough, though, you can find some really neat stuff. There's a jukebox, for instance, and an old fencing outfit, and a surfboard with a picture of a rattlesnake wearing sunglasses on it. I don't know why nobody ever buys these things.

The reason I live with my grandfather is that my mom and dad died in a car accident the day after I was born. Whenever I tell people about this—mainly grown-ups—they end up looking at either the floor or the ceiling and they always say, "I'm sorry." I'm not sure what they have to be sorry about, though. My parents died before I ever got to know them. I guess that makes me an orphan, technically, but it's not something I spend any time thinking about.

My grandfather was on the phone with some-body when I got home, so I went straight to my bedroom and collapsed on my bed. After the assembly at school, I had asked Kevin Applebab if he had noticed anything unusual about Howard Thigpen, and Kevin Applebab had said, "Yeah, he was kind of screwy, wasn't he? *I am Howard Thigpen! I control the universe! I eat money for breakfast! Watch me as I rub this fifty-dollar bill all over my body!*"

"No, I mean did you notice anything about the way he looked?"

"Why? Was his zipper undone?"

It turned out that nobody I asked had noticed anything at all strange about Howard Thigpen. When I mentioned the sparks of light in his shadow, people just looked at me like I was crazy. Maybe I had been hallucinating when I saw them, but I didn't think so.

I had some math homework to do, so I sat at my desk for half an hour with my calculator and a pencil. I'm pretty good at math, but I've always had trouble multiplying and dividing fractions. I can never remember what I'm supposed to do with the numerators and denominators. My math teacher (who also directs the school play every year) calls it my tragic flaw. Unfortunately, that's exactly what we had been studying for the last few weeks—multiplying and dividing fractions. Our homework was getting more and more complicated every day.

I had finished only about half the problems before I decided to take a break. I went to the kitchen and ate a couple of brownies and drank a glass of milk. I was lucky to find the brownies, since the only snack food my grandfather likes to eat nowadays is cans of mixed nuts, and I've been wary of nuts of all kinds ever since my rotten peanut experience.

I still wasn't quite ready to finish my home-work, so I spent a few minutes puttering around the apartment looking for something to do. I didn't feel like watching TV, and I had already read all my comic books about a dozen times. It was then that I remembered Mr. Fred and the loudspeaker experiment. I found some tape and a straight pin in one of the kitchen drawers, and after a little searching I found a sheet of construction paper inside my desk. I put together a working loud-speaker. It was just like the one I had made in class. I even fastened tape along both sides of the crease, inside and out, so that it wouldn't come undone.

Now all I had to do was find a record album and I would be in business. I knew there were some old disco records locked inside the jukebox downstairs, but I couldn't get to them without the jukebox key. My grandfather keeps the keys for the various antiques in a shoe box beneath the cash register. Unfortunately, he keeps all sorts of other stuff in there, too—rubber bands, washers, old batteries, you name it. Without his help, I would probably never find the right key. Even with his help it might take me hours.

I decided to ask him anyway. When I got downstairs, though, I saw that he was still on the telephone. "Of course it's natural!" he was yelling. "Human beings have been eating meat for three million years, which is about three million years longer than *you've* been around, I should add. You know, you hippies are all alike. What will you do when it's kill or be killed, though, huh? Tell me that! Let's lock you in a cage with a few starving chickens, and we'll see who starts eating meat!"

I could tell from the tone of his voice that my grandfather was arguing with his assistant, Shimerman. Shimerman is not only a vegetarian, which means that he doesn't eat any meat, but he is also a vegan, which means that he doesn't eat any eggs or cheese or butter and he doesn't drink any milk. When he first told me this, I assumed that he must live on salad and baked potatoes and maybe the occasional bran muffin, but I was wrong. He does eat all those things, of course, but he also eats a lot of interesting foods, like couscous and tofu and spicy vegetable curry. Some of these foods are actually pretty tasty—the spicy vegetable curry, for instance, although it's no hamburger.

Shimerman is also really into recycling, which is probably why he took a job in an antique store in the first place. He never throws anything away, and he's always walking around with his arms full of soda cans and paper sacks and all kinds of other stuff he's found in my grandfather's trash cans. That is exactly the sort of thing that causes my grandfather to flip out.

I listened to him shouting, "What do you mean, 'Molars are for grinding berries'? And what are the incisors for? *What about the incisors, Shimerman?* You can't have it both ways, you know."

I had heard my grandfather arguing with Shimerman about a million times, and I knew that this was likely to go on for quite a while. I took my loudspeaker and went back upstairs.

I was just about to get started on my math homework again when I had an idea. It happened while I was staring at the wallpaper above my bed. My wallpaper is corrugated, like the lining of a cardboard box, which means that it has thousands of tiny grooves that run in a straight line from the floor to the ceiling. Wouldn't it be interesting, I thought, if there was *music* locked inside those grooves, just like the music in the grooves of a record album? Then I could follow the grooves with my needle and listen to the music through my loudspeaker.

The whole idea was ridiculous, of course— after all, who would go to the trouble of recording music on some random kid's wall? Still, it was either the wallpaper or the fractions, and I decided I might as well give it a try.

I held the construction-paper loudspeaker cone between my fingers, and I traced one of the grooves in the wallpaper with the needle. All I heard was an extra-loud *skritch*ing noise. It sounded a little like one of Kevin Applebab's hamsters rolling over in his wood shavings. I tested a few more of the grooves just to be on the safe side and heard exactly the same thing—*skritch skritch skritch*. My wallpaper was nothing but regular wallpaper.

Still, I didn't want to give up on the idea so quickly. My grandfather and Shimerman both watch the old black-and-white Sherlock Holmes movies shown on Saturday afternoon TV. It's one of the few things they've ever been able to agree on. I grew up watching these movies with them, and I've always liked to think that there might be clues and hidden messages like that in the real world. I walked around the house looking for other objects that had grooves I could check. The cap on my shampoo bottle gave off a sort of high-pitched squeaking sound. The furrows along the edge of the kitchen table made the same burrowing hamster noise as the wallpaper. The celery in the refrigerator barely made any noise at all, and on top of that it gunked up the tip of the needle so that I had to wipe it clean on my blue jeans.

My blue jeans! I hoisted myself onto the kitchen counter and ran the needle along one of the grooves in the lap of my blue jeans.

This is what I heard: *(skritch skritch) help (skritch) the light from our (skritch skritch skritch)*.

Holy cow!

I tried it again and heard exactly the same message: *(skritch skritch) help (skritch) the light from our (skritch skritch skritch).*

I tested a few of the other grooves and found only static, but fifteen or twenty grooves away from the one I had started with I heard the announcement once again: *(skritch skritch) help (skritch) the light from our (skritch skritch skritch).*

Somebody had recorded a message in the fabric of my blue jeans, and it sounded like that somebody was in trouble!

FOUR

I spent the rest of the evening digging through my dresser to test my other blue jeans. It turned out that I owned seven of them—eight if you count my cut-offs—and each pair had roughly a thousand grooves. You've probably never listened for hidden messages in your blue jeans before, but believe me when I tell you it can take a while. I was so busy that I missed my second-favorite television show, *The Adventures of Pill-Bug Man*, which comes on every Monday night at eight o'clock. *The Adventures of Pill-Bug Man* is about a guy who is bitten by a radioactive pill-bug and develops special pill-bug superpowers. All this really means is that he can curl himself into a ball and roll away when he gets frightened, but he still manages to foil crimes somehow.

I didn't have any luck with my other blue jeans. No matter how carefully I listened to them the only thing I could make out was a sort of stuttery hissing noise. By the time I finished checking the last pair, it was already nine thirty. I microwaved a chicken pot pie and ate it, and then I changed into my pajamas and went to bed. It took me a long time to fall asleep. I kept imagining that I would wake up in the morning and discover that my amazing talking blue jeans had disappeared or unraveled while I was asleep. Eventually I got out of bed and folded them into a square and placed them under my pillow so that I could rest my hand on them. After that I fell straight to sleep.

The first thing I did when I woke up the next morning was unfold the blue jeans and test them again to make sure the announcement was still there. I felt a moment of panic when I didn't hear anything, but then I realized I had put the needle to the wrong groove. I tried again, and the message came rustling out of the loudspeaker: *(skritch skritch) help (skritch) the light from our (skritch skritch skritch)*. I wished I knew some way to decipher the skritches, but I couldn't think of one.

I can't HELP it if THE LIGHT FROM OUR porch is keeping you awake?

It would HELP if you would stop shining THE LIGHT FROM OUR flashlights in our faces?

I would love to HELP you cover THE LIGHT FROM OUR windows, but I'm kind of busy right now?

I had no idea.

My grandfather's assistant, Shimerman, was already working at the front counter when I came downstairs. He was eating handfuls of granola from a paper sack, absentmindedly picking the crumbs that fell onto his shirt and popping them into his mouth. All of his shirts are the same mottled shade of gray-pink because he makes them out of the sheets of lint he collects from the dryers at the Laundromat. He spins the yarn and weaves the cloth and everything. Like I said, he's something of a recycling fanatic.

He gave me a salute and said, "Hello, Young Ruggles."

"Hello, Shimerman."

"What's that you're carrying?" he asked.

It was the loudspeaker I had made. I had stowed the blue jeans inside my backpack so that I could show them to Kevin Applebab when I got to school, but I was afraid that if I put the loudspeaker in there the funnel would get crushed. I didn't want to tell Shimerman the whole story, though, so I just said, "Oh, that. Well, Mr. Fred had us make these loudspeakers in science class. Only mine doesn't work so well. There's this static."

Shimerman combed a piece of granola out of his beard. "That might be the construction paper," he said. "You should try using something more durable."

My grandfather shouted down from the kitchen. "Are you talking with the customers again, Shimerman? Shut your trap and get back to work, you lazy, shaggy-haired, good-for-nothing . . ." His voice trailed away.

Shimerman waited as he always did for my grandfather to stop yelling. Then he continued as though he hadn't heard a word. "Maybe I can find something better for you to use. I'll have a look around the store while you're at school." He burped quietly. "Did you know that the first small burp is a sign from your body that you should stop eating? It means that you're officially full. Most people don't realize that."

Shimerman was always coming up with strange little facts like this about the human body. He usually turned out to be right.

"See you later, Shimerman," I said, and I headed out the front door.

My school is only three blocks away from home, and unless the weather is really bad I almost always walk there rather than take the bus. There's something nice about feeling the pavement passing beneath your shoes as you listen to the cars racing one another down the street. I even like the clouds of yellow jackets that hover around the trash cans in the summer, which will generally leave you alone if you don't squirt them with a water gun.

I got to school about ten minutes early. Kevin Applebab wasn't there yet, so I went ahead and took my seat in Mr. Fred's class. In elementary school Kevin and I used to share the same room all day long, but at Howard Thigpen we had only one class together—boys' gym. This was probably for the best. The people at school tended to gawk at the two of us when they saw us hanging out together. I assume this is because I am short and kind of round, as I mentioned, and Kevin Applebab is tall and kind of pointy. Anyway, I wouldn't see him until the fourth period.

Mr. Fred spent the hour teaching us about light rays and how they shift directions when you shoot them through a lens. Our health teacher, Miss Breitweiser, spent the hour reading to us from our health textbook, which is called *Notions in Personal Health: Your Guide to Keeping Fit and Not Smoking*. Our history teacher, Miss Finch, spent the hour reading to us from our history textbook, which is called *200 Years of American History: New and Updated for the Bicentennial*. I kept checking inside my backpack to make sure my blue jeans were still there.

"I've got something important to show you," I said to Kevin Applebab, as we changed into our gym clothes just before fourth period. "You won't believe it when you see it."

"What is it?" he asked.

"A pair of blue jeans," I said.

Kevin Applebab rolled his eyes. "Oh boy. Blue jeans. I should have brought my camera."

"Trust me. These aren't just any blue jeans," I

told him, and then the bell rang. Kevin Applebab and I hurried out of the locker room to line up below the basketball hoop.

"I'll have to show you at lunch," I finished.

If Mr. Fred is my favorite teacher at Howard Thigpen Junior High School, Coach Channering, the gym teacher, is definitely my least favorite. I have four reasons: (#1) He forces the kids in his class to run laps if they aren't waiting beneath the basketball hoop ten seconds after the bell rings. (#2) He has a loud whistle that he likes to blow in our ears just to make us jump. (#3) He smells kind of like a stale ham sandwich, but he's always saying it's someone *else* who must smell like the stale ham sandwich. And (#4), on top of all these things, he has cool nicknames for the kids he likes—Dash and Slick and K-Man, for instance—and insulting nicknames for the kids he doesn't like—Pudgy, Goofball, Sir Droops-a-lot, etc.

I'm not one of the kids he particularly likes, but I'm not one of the kids he particularly dislikes, either. Mostly he just can't remember who I am. Every day when he takes roll and gets to my name, he looks up and down the row for me as if he's never seen me before in his life. He seems completely surprised when I turn out to be who I am.

Tuesday is dodgeball day in gym. We divide into two teams, and when Coach Channering blows his whistle, we have at each other with six foam rubber balls. I can't throw very well, and I can't run very well, and I couldn't dodge anything if you paid me a million dollars—but I can catch better than anybody would guess. The other kids in my class figured this out at the very beginning of the school year. Usually, when we play dodgeball, they will wait until I am the last person left on my team and then throw all six balls at me at once. They know I might be able to catch one or two, but the other four will thump into me before I can grab them. It gets pretty boring watching red balls whizzing back and forth and waiting for the other kids to get pegged so that it will be my turn, but that's exactly what I have to do. You can always tell when a class has been playing dodgeball by all the people walking around school the rest of the day with moon-shaped red marks on their arms or foreheads.

At lunch, I pulled Kevin Applebab outside and

fished the blue jeans from my backpack. "They look like regular blue jeans to me," he said. "I still don't see what the big deal is."

So I told him about the loudspeaker experiment I had tried at home and the rustling sound in the wallpaper and what I discovered when I tested the blue jeans. I made sure no one was looking, and I traced one of the grooves with the needle and played the message for him: *(skritch skritch) help (skritch) the light from our (skritch skritch skritch)*.

I could tell he was impressed. "I'll never doubt you again," he said. He thought about it for a second. "So can you tell what the skritches are saying?"

"No. I must have listened to the message a hundred times. It never gets any clearer."

"What about your other blue jeans? Did you test them?"

"Every pair I own. Nothing."

"Can I borrow the loudspeaker for a minute?" he asked.

When I handed it to him, he began running the needle along the furrows of his own blue jeans—

first the left leg, then the right, and finally the butt. We listened closely for an announcement, but we didn't hear anything very interesting.

An older girl happened by while he was tracing one of the grooves in his back pocket. "Why are you scratching your butt with that needle?" she asked. "Do you have some sort of rash?"

Kevin Applebab froze in place.

"Um . . . yeah . . . poison ivy," he said. "See, I went camping with my Boy Scout troop, and I was sitting on this log. I was wearing my swimsuit. The rash must have started out on the backs of my knees, but it worked its way up, I guess."

The girl shuddered. I got the impression that she was thinking about how much fun she would have telling her friends this story. "Gee," she said, "thanks *so much* for sharing," and she walked away.

Kevin Applebab gave the loudspeaker back to me. "Well, that was embarrassing," he said.

The bell rang for fifth period.

FIVE

Kevin Applebab and I decided that we would get together at my house after school to perform a few more tests on my blue jeans. There had to be some way to unscramble the rest of the message, to de-skritch the skritches. We weren't quite sure what we were going to try, but we knew that if we put our minds to it, we were bound to come up with something. The two of us met in the cafeteria after seventh period. A few ninth-grade girls walked by, pointing and giggling at us. Kevin Applebab looked irritated. "People have already started calling me 'Rash Butt,'" he said. "It only took them two hours."

"Don't worry, I'm sure it will go away in a few days."

And then, because I couldn't resist myself, I added, "Like a rash."

He slugged me on the arm. "Very funny," he said.

I bought a snack out of the vending machine before we left for the antique shop, a bag of Thigpen Brand Potato Chips. Howard Thigpen was kind of a jerk, it was true, but his potato chips were a real bargain. Sometimes you will open a bag of chips from a vending machine and find that all the chips have settled to the bottom and the rest of the bag is mostly air. Funyuns are the absolute worst when it comes to this—I once bought a bag of Funyuns that contained only three chips and a couple of leftover crumbs! But Thigpen Brand Potato Chips are always filled right to the top of the bag. Also, they have ridges. Some people don't like ridges, but in my opinion they keep the chips from disintegrating into crumbs, so I'm in favor of them. This particular bag of chips was so full that I saved half of them to eat when I got home. I put the bag in my backpack, nestling it behind my blue jeans.

Kevin Applebab and I stopped at Gadzooks after we left school. Gadzooks is North Mellwood's biggest comic book store. It is only a block from my grandfather's antique store. It stocks hundreds of new comics on wooden shelves in the center of the floor and thousands of old comics in Mylar bags around the walls. It also carries baseball cards and action figures and various gummy animals in plastic bins—gummy bears, gummy worms, etc.

Kevin Applebab and I try to stop in every Tuesday afternoon when the new comics come out. We make a point of buying our comics just as soon as they're on the shelf.

We were in luck. The latest issue of *The Uncanny X-Men* was out, as well as the latest issue of *Fizz and the Amazing Plop*. *The Uncanny X-Men* is my own favorite comic book, and *Fizz and the Amazing Plop* is Kevin's. You've probably heard of *The Uncanny X-Men*—it's about a group of mutants who do battle with super-villains and hide their identities from the regular people who fear and misunderstand them. *Fizz and the Amazing Plop* is fairly new—it's on issue number twelve—and is about an alien force that disguises itself as an Alka-Seltzer tablet. In every issue, the alien force grants a different strange power to whoever swallows it. It also cures that person's indigestion.

We bought our comics and were leaving the

store when who should come through the front door but Mr. Fred. "Dwayne Ruggles! Kevin Applebab!" he said. "What a pleasure to run into you here!"

"What are you doing in Gadzooks, Mr. Fred?" I asked.

"Well, as it happens, I live right upstairs," he said, pointing at the ceiling. "So I'm in here all the time. But to answer your question, I came in today hoping to find the new issues of *The Uncanny X-Men* and *Fizz and the Amazing Plop*."

"You read *The Uncanny X-Men*!?" I asked.

"You read *Fizz and the Amazing Plop*!?" Kevin Applebab asked.

Mr. Fred laughed. "I've been reading *The Uncanny X-Men* since before you were born. The best issues are numbers one-forty through one-eighty. Have you read them?"

I said that I hadn't.

"You can borrow mine sometime, but you have to promise not to bend them or get crumbs on them. And *Fizz and the Amazing Plop*—" He shook his head and gave a long whistle. "Truly groundbreaking. The way the action of the story spills right over into the Alka-Seltzer advertisements, I've never seen anything like it."

We loved Mr. Fred. "I guess we'll see you in class tomorrow," I told him.

"Okay, I'll see you boys later," he said.

When we left the store, he was walking back and forth between the shelves of new releases, thumbing through the stacks for crisp, glossy copies of the comics he wanted to buy.

Kevin Applebab and I headed back to the antique shop. Shimerman was still there. He was bent over behind an antique pile with a dust rag and a bottle of all-purpose wood-and-metal polish. My grandfather was behind the front counter selling a wicker footstool to a woman in a polka-dot dress. "What do you mean, 'How do I know if it works?'" he was saying. "It's a footstool, for crying out loud!"

"I was just wondering if—"

"Look, if it holds your feet up, it works. There's nothing complicated about it. It's not like there's a motor inside the thing."

We waved to my grandfather as we squeezed between the antiques on our way to my bedroom, but I don't think he noticed us. We were halfway up the staircase when Shimerman came rumbling up behind us. "Young Ruggles!" he called out, and Kevin Applebab and I turned around.

"I didn't see you come in," Shimerman said. He was breathing hard. "I did some digging while you were gone, like I promised, and I found something for you. I almost missed it, but I looked beneath a pile of toasters and the bumper of a '57 Buick, and there it was. Follow me." Shimerman led us to the back corner of the antique store. He gestured at an oddly shaped box that he had covered with a particularly filthy bath towel. "Voilà," he said, and he pulled the bath towel away.

It was an old Victrola record player, the kind with a crank on the side and a long brass horn. I had seen a picture of one once in an encyclopedia. In the old days, if you wanted to play a record, you had to wind the crank, which would spin the turntable, and then you had to place the needle to the groove of the record. The needle was connected to the long brass horn, and the music would come pouring out of the opening. It was a lot like the loudspeakers we had made in Mr. Fred's class. Shimerman ran his finger around the lip of the horn, which was split into four segments that curled over on themselves like the petals of a tulip. "This should work much better than that thing you made out of construction paper," he said. "All you have to do is unscrew the horn, and there you have it."

"It's perfect," I said. "Thank you, Shimerman."

"Happy to help," he said. He fished a screwdriver out of the Jamaican satchel he always carried around with him and tossed it to me. "Good luck."

Kevin Applebab and I ran through the next half hour fiddling with the screws that joined the horn to the base of the Victrola. Nobody had removed them since the record player had been put together seventy or eighty years ago—that much was obvious. They were covered with a sort of dull green grit that glued them to the wood. The horn, on the other hand, was spotless. Shimerman must have polished it before we came home, because I could see a stretched-out image of my face reflected in the metal.

Eventually, Kevin Applebab and I managed to work the screws loose. We detached the horn from the record player and carried it upstairs. The needle was fixed to the narrow end, just like the needle I had joined to my construction paper loudspeaker, only a lot more securely. I had to be careful not to prick myself with it as I held the horn in my hand. The first thing we did when we got to my bedroom was dig out the blue jeans from my backpack and test the Victrola horn on them. We spread them out perfectly flat on top of my desk and traced the groove with the needle, listening carefully.

Sure enough, the skritches were gone. The message was as clear as sunshine. What it said was this: *Please. You must help us. He's stealing the light from our eyes.*

Kevin Applebab and I yelled together in triumph. We spent a few minutes leaping around on my bed like little kids, hooting and pumping our arms. We couldn't help ourselves.

Then we played the announcement once again. *Please. You must help us. He's stealing the light from our eyes.*

I think we both realized how baffled we were at exactly the same time.

We looked at each other. "We still have a problem, don't we?" Kevin Applebab said.

I frowned. "'He's stealing the light from our eyes'? What on earth could that mean?"

"And who's this 'he' they're talking about?" Kevin Applebab said.

"And how are we supposed to help them when we don't even know who they are?" I said.

Suddenly we were both exhausted. This happens to me. I will have a great explosion of energy for a few minutes and then, wham!—I will feel like I haven't slept in days. I never know where it comes from. We both lay down on the floor for a while staring at the ceiling. We could hear the bell dinging downstairs as someone opened the front door. A bird whistled outside my window. Finally Kevin Applebab said, "I think I need something to eat. I'm about to faint here."

"Me, too. I don't know what happened."

I worked my hand into my backpack and found the bag of Thigpen Brand Potato Chips. Kevin Applebab and I began sharing them. I was just sort of fooling around, not thinking about anything in particular, when I ran the horn of the Victrola along the ridge in one of the chips.

Room 422, the chip said.

Kevin Applebab and I were astonished. "Do that again," he said.

I tried, but the chip just made a grainy *shishing* noise. "It's gone," I said.

"Where did it go?" Kevin asked. "What did you do with it?"

"I didn't do anything. I don't know."

We went through the bag testing the ridges on every single chip, but we didn't have any luck. It wasn't until we reached the very last one that we heard the message a second time: *Room 422*. Again, though, it disappeared after the first listen.

It took us a while to figure out what had happened. The reason the words were vanishing from the chips so quickly was that the needle was scraping the ridges clean. The swerves and ripples that carried the sound were being ground away into tiny crumbs.

It was then that Kevin Applebab had his flash

of inspiration. "Hey, what brand are those blue jeans of yours?" he said.

I tugged them down from the top of my desk and read the label on the tag:

THIGPEN BRAND BLUE JEANS

33 RESERVOIR ROAD, NORTH MELLWOOD, U.S.A.

I looked at Kevin Applebab. Kevin Applebab looked at me.

"I think we just got our first clue," he said.

SIX

It was getting late, and Kevin Applebab had to get home for supper. His parents are really strict when it comes to things like that—curfews and mealtimes and such. Unfortunately, his mom is a terrible cook. She has some secret ingredient that she uses in all her meals which makes them taste like pickled beets (maybe the secret ingredient *is* pickled beets, although I don't know for sure). Still, she insists that the entire family gather at the dinner table at six o'clock every night no matter what the food is about to taste like. Whenever I spend the night with him, Kevin and I always beg her to let us order pizza.

Anyway, we decided before he left that we would skip school the next day to see what we could find out about Howard Thigpen and his factories. We didn't have any tests to worry about, and we figured it would be an easy enough thing to meet in the courtyard before the first bell rang and just take off. There was always a lot of commotion as the cars and buses pulled into the parking lot, and nobody was likely to notice us. We would wait for each other beside the bicycle racks and then make our way to the factory at 33 Reservoir Road.

My grandfather and I ordered takeout that night from Charlie's Dim Sum and Then Some, the Chinese restaurant across the street. We are Charlie's best customers, and he always gives us extra packets of soy sauce and ginger when we come in to pick up an order. My grandfather and I don't particularly like soy sauce and ginger, but Charlie always seems so happy to dump the condiment tray upside down and pour the packets into our bag that we never have the heart to tell him so. We have devoted an entire kitchen drawer to them, along with the occasional ketchup and mustard packet from the Burger Barn.

While we were eating, I asked my grandfather what he knew about Howard Thigpen.

"Howard Thigpen!" he said. "Don't get me started on Howard Thigpen! Let me tell you something, Dwayne. You know all those lunatics who are always going on about how rich people are ruining the world? Well, Howard Thigpen is the sort of rich person who makes them look right."

"What do you mean?" I asked.

"What do I mean about what?"

"About Howard Thigpen," I said.

"Howard Thigpen!" my grandfather said. "Don't get me started on Howard Thigpen! You know, I used to fish in the Mellwood Reservoir before he and his factories scared all the fish away. I used to hike in the Mellwood Woods before he and his factories ripped down all the trees. And the way those employees of his are always wandering around town like a bunch of zombies! It's enough to make you long for the days of the Mellstock Festival—hippies camped up and down the reservoir, electric music blaring at all hours. You know I'm no friend to the hippies, Dwayne, but at least they recognized the value of fresh water when they had it, even if they didn't have enough sense to bathe in it." He shook his head. "'It is easier for a hippie to pass through the eye of a needle than for a rich man to enter into the kingdom of heaven,'" he quoted.

After we had finished dinner, my grandfather went to his bedroom to do some reading, and I decided to spend a little time researching Howard Thigpen on the Internet. My Internet address is dwayneruggles2@aol.com. I have always assumed this must mean there is a dwayneruggles1@aol.com out there somewhere. I would like to meet him. I can't help but wonder whether he is anything like me—a turnip-shaped kid with a comic book collection and a cranky grandfather. The world is a big place, and you never know. I logged onto the Web site of the *Greater Mellwood Bugle*, our local newspaper, and performed a word search for Howard Thigpen. Right away I found four headlines. The first three were—

INDUSTRIALIST TO OPEN SEVEN FACTORIES

NORTH MELLWOOD TO MANUFACTURE BLUE JEANS, POTATO CHIPS, TENNIS SHOES, TOOTHBRUSHES, CANDY BARS, SHAVING CREAM, PIGPENS

and

THIGPEN CORPORATION STRIPS HILLSIDE WEST OF RESERVOIR, ANGERS ENVIRONMENTALISTS

and

JUNIOR HIGH FOOTBALL TEAM RENAMED FOR LOCAL INDUSTRIALIST, WILLIAM HENRY HARRISON "WILDCATS" TO BECOME HOWARD THIGPEN "ROBBER BARONS"

Each of the headlines was illustrated with a picture of Howard Thigpen wearing what looked like a rhinestone jacket. In the first picture he was shaking hands with an extremely skinny bald man in front of an American flag—there were only a few dozen rhinestones on his jacket, scattered here and there like stars on a cloudy night. You could see every single one of them glinting in the sun-light. In the second picture he was standing beside a row of tree stumps, proudly displaying a chain saw, and his jacket was studded with about twice as many rhinestones as before. They stretched all the way from his waist to his collar. In the third picture he was hunched over a football like a center waiting to give a snap, and there were so many rhinestones on his jacket that you could barely even see the fabric.

The fourth headline was—

THIGPEN INVOLVED IN ALTERCATION AT LOCAL HABERDASHERY
"HE DEMANDED MORE RHINESTONES," SAYS TAILOR

Howard Thigpen was not visible at all in this particular photograph. Instead, there was a police officer holding up what must have been his rhinestone jacket, only the photographer had used a flashbulb and the rhinestones had caught the glare. The jacket looked like nothing more than a jacket-shaped section of light.

I tried to access the articles by clicking on the headlines with my cursor, but it turned out that if you actually wanted to read them, you had to give the *Greater Mellwood Bugle* your credit card information. I do not have a credit card, although I receive offers from American Express all the time. I think I must have gotten on some sort of mailing list.

Anyway, I didn't have much luck finding out about Howard Thigpen on the Internet. The Thigpen Corporation Web site was mostly just stock estimates and other financial information, and www.howardthigpen.com was only a catalog of the various products that the Thigpen Corporation sells—candy bars, toothbrushes, etc. In fact, the only thing I found out about Howard Thigpen that I hadn't already known was that he really liked rhinestones for some reason.

Before I turned off the computer, I looked up the word "haberdashery" in the online dictionary. It was just a fancy word for a men's clothing store.

SEVEN

The next morning Kevin Applebab and I met by the bicycle racks in front of the school. We waited until the five-minute bell rang, when all the kids began to head inside. Then we just walked away. Sure enough, nobody noticed us.

I was kind of surprised by how easy the whole thing was. I had never ditched school before, and I kept expecting Principal McNutt or Coach Channering or somebody to tap me on the shoulder and yank me back inside. But the farther we got from the building, the more obvious it became that no one was going to stop us. At one point a police car coasted past us, its lights giving a single blink. My first instinct was to take off running, but Kevin Applebab convinced me to just keep walking along like we were lawyers or grocery store clerks or something—people who were supposed to be there. Eventually the police car made a turn at a stoplight and drove away.

The Mellwood Reservoir was at the other end of town, and we decided that the fastest way to get there would be to take the bus. We wanted the route called Factory Row—it would carry us straight to the west side of the reservoir, where the Thigpen Complex was located. There were bus signs on poles up and down the sidewalk. The times of departure were printed on them in small black letters. We found the first Factory Row stop three or four blocks away from school. The next departure time was in forty-five minutes. We had plenty of time to kill.

"What do you want to do until the bus gets here?" Kevin Applebab asked me.

"I don't know. I guess I could use another breakfast."

"Another breakfast?"

"I had my first breakfast this morning, but I'm still hungry."

There was a bagel restaurant right by the bus stop, and we went inside. I ordered a chocolate chip bagel. I had never eaten a bagel before, although Shimerman had once told me that they tasted like chewy doughnuts. Let me just say that if you ever bite into a bagel expecting a chewy doughnut, you're going to be unpleasantly surprised. Mine reminded me of a big soft pretzel without the salt. I had to gnaw on every bite for a full minute before I was able to swallow. It was exhausting just eating the thing. I certainly wasn't hungry anymore by the time I finished.

We were getting ready to leave when a girl about our age came through the door. I recognized her from school. It was the girl in the green army jacket, the same one who had spun the imaginary hula hoop during the assembly on Monday. When she got to the front counter, she asked for "her usual," and the man at the cash register said, "One sesame seed bagel with cream cheese and one double-foam cappuccino, coming right up." He prepared her bagel for her, sealed it in a paper bag, and then poured her a cup of coffee from a machine that made grinding and hissing noises. He handed her order to her, and she headed for the front door. When she saw us at our table, she stopped.

"Hey," she said, "you guys go to Howard

Thigpen." She pulled out a chair and sat down. "Why aren't you in school?" she asked.

Kevin Applebab gave me a look. "Why aren't *you* in school?" he asked her.

"It's Wednesday," she said. "I give myself Wednesdays off." She pulled the sesame seed bagel out of her bag and began to eat it, then took a sip of her double-foam cappuccino. "My name's Emily Holmes," she said. "I love the bagels here, don't you?"

"I was underwhelmed," I had to confess.

"You're crazy," she told me. "They're the best in town." She took another bite of her bagel and made a noise with a lot of *m*'s in it. I could tell she wasn't pretending; she was really enjoying herself. "So are you going to tell me your names or what?"

"Dwayne Ruggles," I said.

"Kevin Applebab," said Kevin.

"And why did you say you weren't in school?"

I barely knew this girl, and I certainly wasn't going to tell her about the loudspeaker, the blue jeans, and the potato chips. Instead I said, "We're doing a research project on Howard Thigpen."

She grimaced. "That guy. Did you know he

made me spin an imaginary hula hoop?"

"Yeah, we were there," said Kevin Applebab.

"I'm not even sure why I did it." She shook her head. She was already finished with her bagel, and she wadded her wax paper into a ball and stuffed it back inside the paper bag. "I have to say, a bagel restaurant is a pretty strange place to conduct research."

"Actually, we're heading down to the factories," I said. "We're about to catch the bus. We have permission."

She stared out the window for a few seconds. She looked like she was watching something that was levitating in midair—a hummingbird, maybe, or Storm from the X-Men. Then she clapped her hands together. "I'll go with you," she announced.

Kevin Applebab and I were stunned by how quickly all this had happened. It would be much harder for us to find out where the messages had come from with somebody who didn't even know about them tagging along, but I could tell that Emily Holmes had made up her mind, and I knew somehow that she would be coming with us one way or the other. She was that sort of person.

There was nothing I could do but say, "Okay."

A few minutes later the three of us caught the bus to Factory Row. The bus itself was kind of dilapidated. The whole thing bounced around like a carnival ride every time we hit a pothole, and the seats smelled kind of like wet tennis shoes, even though it wasn't raining.

It turned out that Emily Holmes was Cinnamon Holmes's younger sister. Cinnamon Holmes was the best babysitter I ever had. When I was a little kid, she used to tell me stories about trolls and elves and hobbits. Once, when she was boiling hot dogs for my dinner, she poured a can of Sprite into the water to try to make the hot dogs fizzy. She was always doing things like that. She went away to college when I was in the fourth grade, but I had never forgotten her, and I told Emily so.

"Thanks," she said. "Cinnamon's studying musical theater now. She's coming home in a few weeks for a visit."

"Tell her Dwayne Ruggles said hi."

"I will," said Emily. "Hmm, Dwayne Ruggles. She used to talk about you all the time, but I never knew who you were before. You were her favorite babysitting kid."

That made me feel good, but I didn't want to sound like I was bragging, so I kept quiet.

The bus rolled past Larry Boone Elementary School, the North Mellwood Shopping Mall, and the Ford Madox Ford Dealership. Every so often it would stop for a passenger, and the brakes would make a terrible squealing noise. They sounded like a rat being tortured into a microphone. I had taken the books out of my backpack so that I could fit the Victrola horn and the blue jeans inside, and I was carrying the entire package in my lap. Whenever the bus slowed down or sped up, I felt the Victrola horn rocking to one side and then settling back in place.

After about ten minutes, I saw the glint of water through the window. The road we were driving on curved around a grassy hill, and a row of seven brick-shaped buildings came into view behind a chain-link fence. It was the Thigpen Corporation Factory Complex.

The bus driver dropped us off by a sign that said—

ALL THIGPEN EMPLOYEES
FOLLOW BLACK ARROW
TO SECURITY CHECKPOINT ➜

We fell in line behind the other passengers—all of them factory workers, I guessed. It was only a few minutes after nine o'clock. The work day must have just been beginning. The group of us walked slowly toward the entrance, which was a swinging iron gate next to a checkpoint about the size of a phone booth. Each of the factory workers stopped beside the checkpoint until the gate opened, and then hurried through before it wheeled shut behind them.

"So what exactly are you guys researching anyway?" Emily Holmes asked as we waited for our turn.

"Blue jeans," I said.

"Potato chips," said Kevin Applebab.

"We're researching blue jeans and potato chips," I said. "What we want to find out, I guess, is how they get those ridges in them. Also, we're looking for a room."

Emily Holmes rolled her eyes. "Obviously

you've planned this down to the smallest detail," she said.

When we got to the iron gate, we found a man standing inside the small building. He was visible only from the waist up, and he wore a silver badge with the word SECURITY printed on it. On the other side of his shirt was a name tag that read HI! MY NAME IS EARL. He had the bushiest beard I had ever seen in my life. "ID cards," he said.

"What?"

"I can't let you in until you show me your ID cards."

I decided to improvise. "We left our ID cards in our lockers. Come on, Earl—it's me, Clarence. The Boss Man will have our tails if we're late today."

The security guard narrowed his eyes at me and began to chuckle. I couldn't see his mouth moving, but his entire beard shook like one of those creepers of gray moss that hang from the telephone wires you see on your way to Disney World. "Nice try, kid. But you're not getting in without ID cards." He jerked his thumb toward the bus stop. "Beat it."

It looked like this was going to be more difficult than I had thought.

As Kevin Applebab, Emily Holmes, and I walked away from the gate, I heard the security guard muttering "Boss Man" to himself, and then "Clarence," and giving a loud, barking laugh.

"Maybe there's some other way inside," I said when the three of us had made it back to the sidewalk. "We could try circling around the fence and looking for a hole."

"You guys didn't really get permission to be here, did you?" Emily Holmes asked.

Kevin Applebab took over. "We got permission from the school, but we forgot to check with the Thigpen people."

"That's right," I said. "I thought Kevin was going to call them, and he thought I was going to call them, and in the end it just slipped our minds."

I don't think Emily Holmes believed us, but she didn't argue.

We decided to hike around the fence and hunt for a second entrance. We walked along the sidewalk in front of the factory complex for a while.

The fence was way too high to climb, and even if it hadn't been, the diamonds between the chain-links were too narrow for us to fit our feet into them. When it cut away from the road over a grassy hill, we followed it. The hill was covered with roots and flattened tree stumps. They were impossible to see in the tall grass until you were right on top of them, and we kept stumbling over them and crashing into one another. I had read somewhere that grass like this makes a perfect home for snakes, and I couldn't stop worrying that we were going to be attacked by one. We were almost ready to give up and turn around when we found a way inside.

There was a creek bed that passed right underneath the fence. It hadn't rained for a few weeks, so the creek was almost perfectly dry, and it wasn't hard for Kevin Applebab and then Emily Holmes to squeeze through the gap between the ground and the fence. I myself had a little more trouble owing to my shape, which, as I mentioned before, is round. One of the fence wires snagged on my shirt. I tugged at it a few times, but it wouldn't come loose. "You're going to have to unhook me,"

I said to Kevin Applebab. He reached down and pulled the end of the wire free.

I wriggled through the opening, stood up, and brushed the dirt off my clothes. The first of the factory buildings was only a few yards away, and there was no one else in sight. We had made it!

"For a minute there, I really thought I was going to get stuck," I said, shaking a few blades of grass from my hair.

Then the alarm bell went off.

EIGHT

Before we knew it, we were surrounded by factory workers. I was sure they were going to drag us
away and beat us up and then call the police or our
parents. But instead they just stood there. They
didn't talk or joke around with one another or anything like that. Their eyes seemed glazed over and
flat, almost without color. Occasionally, one of
them would smooth the sweat back from his forehead with his palm, but that was about it. I wasn't
sure they even noticed us.

The whole experience gave me the willies. In
any case, I didn't move a muscle, and neither did
Kevin Applebab or Emily Holmes. A few minutes
later, the factory bell jangled once more, and the
workers all filed back inside. The courtyard was
empty again.

None of us quite knew what to say. We stared
at one another. A shiver twisted its way up my

spine, and then jumped into Emily Holmes, and from her into Kevin Applebab. Eventually, Kevin Applebab broke the silence. "You know, the factory bell sounds just like the bell at school."

"I noticed the same thing," I said.

"That's why schools have bells in the first place," Emily Holmes said. "At the beginning of the last century, the factory owners had bells installed in the schools to prepare kids for life in the workplace. One bell rings and you have to start working, another bell rings and you have to stop working—that sort of thing. I read about it in one of my sister's books."

We talked about bells for a minute or two, and about Howard Thigpen, and about how schools can be like factories, until we slowly started to feel normal again. Then we decided to begin exploring the factory complex. We figured the blue jeans factory would be the best place to start. At first, we weren't quite sure which building it was in. Luckily, Kevin Applebab noticed that all of the buildings had numbers above the front doors, 1 through 7. Beneath the numbers were signs listing the product each building manufactured—

CANDY BARS, **TOOTHBRUSHES**, etc. The **BLUE JEANS** were in building number 5.

We crossed the courtyard until we got to building number 5. We made sure we stayed in the shade of the factories, and we glanced from side to side every so often to make sure no one was watching us. The door was unlocked, and we slipped inside without any trouble.

The first thing we had to do was cover our ears. The noise was unimaginable! It was a sort of rattling and booming sound, with a terrible sawlike shriek just underneath. There are kids at school who like to listen to music that sounds kind of like this. They play it on their headphones between classes. I myself prefer bands like Duran Duran and the Beach Boys—the classics.

Kevin Applebab tapped me on the shoulder. "Over there!" he shouted.

I could barely hear him, but my eyes followed where his finger was pointing. In the open space of the factory there was a long row of shiny metal machines making pounding and stitching motions. There was a machine that was unspooling zippers from a sort of zipper wheel and attaching them to the blue jeans that were sliding by on a conveyer belt. There was a machine that was punching buttons into the waists of the same blue jeans. There was a machine that was sewing pockets onto the front of the blue jeans and then flipping them over and sewing more pockets onto the back. Above each of the machines was a sign that told you what the machine was designed to do: **ZIPPER MACHINE**, **BUTTON MACHINE**, and **POCKET MACHINE**.

If nothing else, I could tell that Howard Thigpen was extremely organized.

Standing in front of each machine was a factory worker wearing a hard hat, earplugs, and protective goggles. Every so often one of these workers would press a button or pull a lever or untangle a pair of blue jeans that had become caught up in the gears, but mostly they just stood there and watched the blue jeans go gliding past. It must have been like staring at an old, broken television screen with a picture that keeps rotating from the top to the bottom, I thought. I would have been bored out of my mind.

I crooked my neck so that I could see to the very beginning of the row, and there I spotted a sign that said **GROOVE MACHINE**. "That must be it!" I shouted to Emily Holmes and Kevin Applebab. "Come on!"

The three of us made our way along the concrete aisle toward the Groove Machine. None of the workers said anything to us or even looked up from the conveyer belt. It was almost as if they were hypnotized. Of course, it was possible they just didn't hear us, because, as I mentioned before, it was pretty loud inside the factory.

The Groove Machine must have been one of the earliest stages of the blue jeans manufacturing process. It was made up of hundreds of metal tines that reached down onto the conveyer belt and combed through the threads of the blue jeans. The tines looked like the teeth of a rake or the metal prongs of the lie-detector devices they use on TV cop shows. Long strands of blue thread passed through them, and the tines twitched and vibrated and sewed the threads together into blue jeans. Where every tine had been, a groove appeared.

I pulled at the sleeve of the man who was watching the machine. He was standing with his hand balanced over a large red button that read

PRESS THIS BUTTON IN CASE OF THREAD SNARL. Obviously he was paying very close attention to the machine, because it took him a long time to look away from the tines and glance down at me.

"We got your message!" I yelled.

I heard Emily Holmes say, "What message?" to Kevin Applebab. Kevin Applebab held up a finger asking her to wait. The man who was standing over the button, though, didn't seem to hear me at all. He just shrugged his shoulders and shook his head. Then his eyes lost focus and he turned back to the machine.

I tugged at his sleeve again. "Aren't you the guy that works the Groove Machine?"

He came out of his fog and inspected me. "The what?" he shouted, cupping his hand to his ear.

"The Groove Machine," I said.

"The Ovaltine?"

"No, no. The Groove Machine!"

He stared at me blankly for a moment. Then he pointed to a hallway at the far end of the factory and said, "The bathrooms are over there."

This was getting frustrating. I unzipped my backpack and took out the Thigpen Brand Blue

Jeans I had brought. "Look! Did you make these blue jeans?" I asked him.

He shook his head. "I'm new!" he shouted. "I've only been at this station for a month! The guy who used to man the Groovinator was transferred to potato chips! Ned Something-or-other! Hajimura, I think!"

"Thanks!" I shouted.

Once again he must not have heard me properly, because he looked confused and said, "Not until the hot dogs are ready!" Then he blinked a few times, and his gaze drifted back to the Groove Machine.

I decided that I had gotten about all I was going to get out of him. I headed back up the aisle with Kevin Applebab and Emily Holmes. The three of us found a corner of the factory where nobody was working and huddled together so that we could talk without yelling too loud. "Did you guys follow all that?" I asked.

"Most of it," said Kevin Applebab.

"All except the part about the message," said Emily Holmes.

"Maybe this Ned Hajimura fellow is the one

we're looking for," I said. "Does anybody remember which building the potato chip factory is in?"

"It was building number two, I think," Emily Holmes said. "Over that way."

She pointed to a sign posted above a door at the other end of the blue jeans factory. **TO BUILDINGS 4–3–2–AND–1**, it said. We followed it.

Building number 4 appeared to be the shaving cream factory. There was a strong smell of peppermint in the air, which is the Thigpen Brand Shaving Cream trademark scent. Various machines were stirring big vats of blue-green goo, pumping the goo into metal canisters, and pasting labels onto the canisters. As in the blue jeans factory, the factory workers mostly just stood there watching the machines run and occasionally pressing a button or yanking a lever. None of them paid the slightest bit of attention to us.

Building number 3 was the pigpen factory. At one end of the room, large plastic shelves slid down a ramp into a single enormous machine that filled almost the entire building. At the other end of the room the shelves came out of the machine bolted together into boxes the size of walk-in closets, with metal doors attached to the front and fat pink pigs painted on the sides. The factory workers in building number 3 had even less to do than the ones in the others. They just stood around like robots while the pigpens popped out of the machine one by one.

Kevin Applebab, Emily Holmes, and I were on our way to the potato chip factory, passing through a storage room for the completed pigpens, when a door opened and a group of people came streaming in from outside. The people were leading a herd of pigs on short leather leashes. Some of the pigs were pink, like the ones painted on the pigpens, but plenty of them were white or brown or even spotted. There were about twenty people, most of whom had two pigs, which made for about sixty individuals altogether, pigs and people included.

At the head of the crowd was Howard Thigpen.

NINE

Emily Holmes, Kevin Applebab, and I ducked into the nearest pigpen. We crouched against the wall and covered our mouths, breathing as quietly as we could. Howard Thigpen must not have spotted us, because he plunged into what sounded like the middle of a long speech. "And here—as promised, gentlemen—is the pride and joy of the Thigpen Corporation, the Thigpen Brand Pigpen. This sturdy pigpen comes equipped with mechanical feeders and manure disposal brushes that take all the muss and fuss out of modern pig breeding. Our space-age plastic walls will keep your pigs warm in the winter and cool in the summer. And as everybody knows, a comfortable pig is a meaty, juicy pig. Yes, sir, you have a question?"

"My operation has more than fifteen hundred head. What I need to know is, how many of them will fit in this here pen of yours?"

"The Thigpen Brand Pigpen is surprisingly spacious," Howard Thigpen answered, "with room for up to fifty large pigs or seventy-five small pigs in every unit. But for customers such as yourself, whose needs are pig-intensive, the Thigpen Corporation manufactures a larger Thigpen Brand Pigpen, capable of holding up to five hundred pigs. Think of it, only three pigpens for all your fifteen hundred pigs! The sturdy roof will keep the rain and snow off your pigs in even the harshest weather, and every pigpen is painted with our trademark pink pig shape, so that you'll never mistake it for a rabbit hutch or a chicken coop."

The door of the pigpen we were hiding in was cracked open, and I decided to risk a peek outside. The people Howard Thigpen was talking to appeared to be farmers. They weren't wearing overalls and straw hats like the farmers in picture books always do, but some of them did have baseball caps with the names of tractors on them or T-shirts that showed the line where their sunburns started. Then, of course, there was the fact that they were all hauling pigs along with them.

Howard Thigpen himself was standing in a

shaft of sunlight, his hands cradled together in front of his chest. He had the same weird sparks spinning through his shadow that I had noticed in the school auditorium.

"But perhaps you gentlemen would like a demonstration," he said. "Between you, I see, you have brought forty pigs, and the pigs you have brought are all exceptionally large. But if you will unleash them for a moment, you will see that the Thigpen Brand Pigpen will accommodate them easily."

The farmers began to unsnap their pigs from their leashes, and I ducked back inside. I was just in time, too, it turned out. As soon as I squatted in the corner, I heard Howard Thigpen marching across the floor in our direction. "This one should do nicely," he said.

The door of our pigpen swung wide open.

"Come on, boys!" I heard the farmers saying to their pigs, and "Get in there!" and "Move those ham hocks!" Before we knew it, we were surrounded by a herd of stumbling, grunting pigs. When the very last pig was inside, the door slammed shut, and the lock clicked into place.

It was fairly dark in the pigpen, but every time I moved I could feel a new set of bristles brushing against my skin. I could tell that the pigs were packed in with us pretty tightly. My grandfather is always telling his assistant Shimerman that he stinks like a fat pig, but to tell you the truth, the pigs didn't really stink that much at all. In fact, they reminded me of the way dirt smells just after it rains, a sort of rich, potatoey smell. Still, it was obvious that most of the pigs didn't know one another, and they definitely seemed confused. They kept nosing around and bumping into the walls. Every few seconds one of them would step on another one's hoof, and that one would nip at the first one's tail, and then both pigs would let out a squeal.

I could barely hear Howard Thigpen over all the noise. I had to press my ear to the wall to listen. "As you see, my friends, your pigs are all packed securely inside the Thigpen Brand Pigpen," he said to the farmers. "Now, ordinarily, when I open the door, a bell would ring and your pigs would file out in an orderly fashion. But because your pigs have not yet been trained, they will ignore the sound of the bell. So we will have to go inside the pigpen to retrieve them."

"Oh, no!" I whispered. "He's coming in! They're going to find us!"

"What are we going to do?" Kevin Applebab whispered back.

"I don't know, I don't know," I said.

"If only we had a chicken with us," Emily Holmes said.

Kevin Applebab and I had no idea what she was talking about. "Huh?"

"It's a little-known scientific fact," she explained. "Pigs hate chickens. They hate the way they look, they hate the way they smell, and they hate the way they taste. That's why farmers never keep pigs and chickens together in the same building, or even within fifty yards of each other if they can help it. Even the *sound* of a chicken will drive the average pig half crazy."

She sighed. "But we don't have a chicken. Or anything that looks or smells or sounds like a chicken. If only we did."

I couldn't believe my luck. "My chicken imitation is my specialty."

"You're kidding, right?" Emily Holmes said.

"Just listen," I told her. I took a deep breath and let loose.

My chicken imitation begins with a soft gurgling sound high in my throat—*"gug-a-lug-a-lug"*—and finishes with a long, loud clucking noise. *"Buk-buk-buk-buk-bukawh!"* I've been working on it ever since I was a little kid, and even people who have listened to a lot of chickens tell me that they have trouble telling it apart from the real thing.

This particular chicken imitation was one of my better efforts, and it definitely caught the pigs' attention. They fell quiet just long enough for me to hear one of the farmers say, "Did somebody bring . . . a *chicken* in here?"

Then the pigs went berserk.

They began barreling around the pigpen looking for the chicken they thought they had heard, slamming against one another whenever they lost their footing. One of them crashed into me so hard that I fell over flat onto my rear end. I knew I would have bruises on my body by the time I got home, and I guessed that Kevin Applebab and

Emily Holmes would, too. The pigs snorted and squealed and even made a sort of angry hissing noise, a sound you would never imagine might come from a pig.

I could hear the walls of the pigpen creaking and straining against their bolts.

The roof wobbled up and down.

"Don't panic, gentlemen!" I heard Howard Thigpen shouting. "Everything will be okay!"

Then one of the pigs ran headlong into the door and it crashed open. The pigs escaped in a stampede. They were still looking for the chicken presumably, but because there was no chicken, I knew they weren't going to find it. Instead, they just ended up hurtling all over the place, banging into one thing and then another.

I could hear the farmers and Howard Thigpen falling down as the pigs bowled them over. "Help!" one of the farmers called out, and "My pig—she's getting away!" and "I'm hit! I'm hit!"

It was time to take our chance.

"Run!" I cried.

Kevin Applebab and Emily Holmes and I dashed out of the pigpen, pushing our way through the pile of pigs and farmers. We flew as quickly as we could from the storage room. I heard someone shout, "Those kids! *They're* the chicken!" but we were already outside.

We ran across the courtyard and slid through the gap beneath the fence. I was sure someone would chase us down, but the farmers, I guess, were too busy trying to catch their pigs, and Howard Thigpen was too busy trying to calm down the farmers.

We didn't stop running until the factories were long out of sight.

TEN

Eventually, we found a bus stop nine or ten blocks away from the Thigpen Complex, and we caught a ride back into North Mellwood. The bus was filled with factory workers who had just gotten off duty. I was pretty sure we had seen several of them just a few hours earlier, but none of them seemed to recognize us.

"So are you guys going to tell me what's really going on?" Emily Holmes asked, as we rolled through the center of town.

Kevin Applebab and I had to whisper together for a few minutes before we decided it was only fair to fill her in. After all, it was her chicken idea that had saved us from the situation in the pigpen, and we figured she had earned the truth. Besides, we could tell she wasn't going to stop asking questions until she knew everything.

I told her the whole story from beginning to

end—from the sparks I had noticed in Howard Thigpen's shadow to the message I had discovered in my blue jeans, from the horn that Kevin Applebab and I had unscrewed from the Victrola to the second message we had found in the ridges of the potato chips—everything up to the moment when she had bumped into us in the bagel restaurant. "And then there are the rhinestones," I said.

"The rhinestones?" Kevin Applebab was confused. "What rhinestones?"

"That's right!" I said. "I forgot to tell you! I found a few old pictures of Howard Thigpen on the Internet. He used to wear this rhinestone jacket all the time. As far as I can tell, he just kept adding rhinestones to it until there was no place left to fit them. He wanted to put even more of them on there, but he couldn't because there wasn't any room. Then he flipped out or something. Anyway, he doesn't wear the thing anymore. Maybe the police confiscated it. I don't know for sure."

By this time we were at the other end of North Mellwood, pulling up outside the bagel restaurant. We got out of the bus and began to walk home. It turned out that Emily Holmes lived only a few blocks away from me, in an apartment halfway between the school and my grandfather's antique shop. Kevin Applebab lived in roughly the same neighborhood, in a two-story house that had a tire swing in the front yard.

We were passing by one of those office buildings that has mirrors in place of all its windows when Emily Holmes grabbed my arm. "Wait up," she said. "We need to go inside for a minute." Kevin Applebab and I followed her through the lobby of the office building, past the elevators and the bathrooms and the water fountains, to a long row of vending machines.

They were easily the most impressive vending machines I had ever seen. There were at least a dozen of them, and they were so tall that I couldn't see the top level of products inside without jumping up into the air. There were machines for candy bars and cookies and potato chips, a machine that poured soft drinks into milk-jug-sized paper cups (one button even said COKE--SUNKIST–DR PEPPER SUICIDE), and a machine filled with canned sodas I had never even heard of, including a Japanese drink called King Bubble that came in both strawberry and sweet green tea flavors. There was even a machine stocked entirely with snack foods for vegetarians— granola bars, sunflower seeds, and dried fruits and vegetables. I made a mental note to tell Shimerman about it.

"These are the fanciest and most popular vending machines in town," Emily Holmes told us. "One of my uncles works for the vending machine company, and he says that they pay him to restock the machines here every day. The ones at school they only restock on Friday afternoons."

"This was good thinking," I said. "I haven't had anything to eat since that terrible bagel this morning."

Kevin Applebab nodded. "Yeah, I'm starving."

"No, no, no," Emily Holmes said. "You guys don't get it. The Thigpen Brand Potato Chips you bought at school yesterday are at least a few days old. The ones in here are brand-new. We can see if the message has changed."

She slipped three quarters into the vending machine and down fell a bag of Thigpen Brand

Potato Chips. "Did you bring that Victrola horn with you?" she asked me.

"It's in my backpack," I said.

"Let me see it."

When I handed it over to her, she opened the bag, took a chip out, and ran the needle along one of the ridges. Right away we heard a new message: *Please hurry. Room 422. I'm the last one.*

Emily Holmes was so surprised that she almost dropped the Victrola horn. She lifted both her eyebrows and said, "Okay, you're not crazy. I wasn't so sure until now."

"Try it again," I said.

As with the chips from the previous bag, the message inside the ridge had already disintegrated into crumbs. But every single chip in the bag contained exactly the same plea for help. We listened to it over and over again: *Please hurry. Room 422. I'm the last one.*

Ned Hajimura had obviously been busy.

ELEVEN

It was almost five thirty, and after we had finished listening to and eating the last of the potato chips, we decided to call it quits for the day. Our families would almost certainly be wondering why we weren't home yet, and we didn't want them to get suspicious and start asking questions. Just before we went our separate ways, we talked about it and decided that it would be a bad idea to miss classes two days in a row. We agreed to meet by the school auditorium during lunch the next day to figure out what we were going to do next.

That night, my grandfather and I ate our left-over Chinese food from Charlie's Dim Sum and Then Some, and afterward I got to watch my favorite television show. My favorite television show is about a retired barbarian named Yor who is living out his old age in sunny Fort Lauderdale, Florida. Yor carries a sword and a crossbow on his back, and he wears a helmet with two big horns sticking out of it, but other than that he is just a regular retired guy. Occasionally a villain from his past will show up in Fort Lauderdale, and Yor will have to do battle with him, but usually he just plays shuffleboard with his buddy Rudy. At the end of every episode he sits by a pond and tosses bread crumbs to the ducks. The show is called *The Happy, Golden Days of Yor*.

A few minutes after the episode was over, Kevin Applebab called me on the phone and said, "Are you watching channel seventeen? You have to turn to channel seventeen."

I switched the station over and caught the second half of a news bulletin. "—oward Thigpen. Though their identities are unknown, the Thigpen Corporation has released the following composite sketches of the children, based on eyewitness descriptions by the farmers who own the pigs."

A set of three drawings appeared on the screen: a dark-haired girl in a green army jacket, a tall, skinny kid in a *Fizz and the Amazing Plop* T-shirt, and a short, lightbulb-shaped kid wearing a backpack—Emily Holmes, Kevin Applebab, and me. Kevin Applebab had a much bigger nose than he has in real life, and for some reason I was carrying a baseball bat, but other than that the likenesses were pretty accurate.

"In other news," the announcer continued, "a thunderstorm looks likely to reach North Mellwood by late Friday night, and the temperature is expected to—"

I turned the volume down. "How many people do you think saw that?" I asked.

"Well, they were interrupting a rerun of *Barney Miller*, and almost nobody watches reruns of *Barney Miller*, so probably not too many," Kevin Applebab said. "But still . . ."

"Still . . ." I let my voice trail off. "I wonder if any of the other stations ran the same news bulletin."

"I was just asking myself the same question," Kevin Applebab said. "Take a look at channel four."

I changed the station and turned the volume back up. Howard Thigpen was standing in front of a blue curtain saying, "We only want the children for questioning, of course. However, I do remind you that at least one of them is capable of imitating a chicken, so they should be approached with—"

I was having a difficult time listening to him. I kept watching the fireworks display of light in his shadow. It had become harder and harder for me to ignore it ever since I realized it was there. "Can't you see that?" I asked Kevin Applebab. "Those lights in his shadow. Look closely."

"Hey! Now that you mention it, there *is* something there." He made a surprised sound. "There are a bunch of lights. They're sort of darting around like fireflies. Is that what you see?"

"Exactly," I said. "But I can't figure out where they come from." Suddenly, I had a troubling idea—or the beginning of one at least. "Hey, do you remember the message we found in the blue jeans?"

"Yeah."

"What were the exact words?"

"'Please,'" Kevin Applebab quoted. "'You must help us. He's stealing the light from our eyes.'"

"'The *light* from our *eyes*,'" I repeated. "'He's stealing the *light* from our *eyes*.'"

The mystery was getting weirder and weirder.

We sat quietly for a minute, trying to fit all the pieces together, until the TV caught our attention again.

"—two pigs are still missing, and we can only presume that they are loose somewhere inside the factories," Howard Thigpen finished. The screen went black as the TV station switched to a commercial.

TWELVE

As it turned out, Emily Holmes, Kevin Applebab, and I did not get the chance to meet during lunch the next day. Kevin and I were in our fourth period gym class heaving something called a medicine ball back and forth when the office monitor came in and handed a note to Coach Channering. A medicine ball is a stuffed brown leather thing not much bigger than a soccer ball, but it weighs about as much as a microwave oven. When you play basketball, you get to dribble and shoot and try to slam-dunk the ball. When you play volleyball, you get to bump the ball into the air with your fists and smack it over the net. But as far as I can tell, the only object to playing with a medicine ball is to try not to pull your arm out of its socket.

Anyway, Coach Channering read the note the office monitor had given him and then pointed at Kevin Applebab. "You. Twig-boy. Principal McNutt wants you to report to his office." He glanced at the note again and said, "I don't think this other boy is here. Has anybody seen Dwayne Ruggles?" he shouted.

"I'm Dwayne Ruggles," I told him.

He looked me up and down as though he didn't quite believe me. "Well, I guess you wouldn't have any reason to lie about it, would you. Report to the office with Twig-boy. On the double."

Kevin Applebab and I changed out of our gym clothes in the locker room and then went straight to Principal McNutt's office. It was the first time either of us had ever been there. Usually it was the same few kids who got sent to the principal's office every week, kids who got caught smoking or fighting or flipping somebody off in the hallway. It was against the law for principals to paddle students in North Mellwood, but I was still worried.

Emily Holmes was already waiting in the office when we went in. She was sitting in a large padded chair. Principal McNutt told us to sit down in the chairs on either side of her. I looked around at the room—at the bowl full of marbles on Principal McNutt's desk, the college certificates on his wall, the Historic Landmarks of North Mellwood calendar, and the shelf full of books with titles like *Junior High School Administration for Dummies* and *Kids Who Don't Smoke Go to College*.

"This fax came in half an hour ago," Principal McNutt began. "Why don't you children take a look at it?"

He passed it to Kevin Applebab, who passed it to Emily Holmes, who passed it to me. It was the same set of drawings we had seen on the news the night before, along with the following statement:

THESE SUSPECTS ARE WANTED

FOR QUESTIONING BY

THE THIGPEN CORPORATION

IN THE MATTER OF

BREAKING AND ENTERING AND/OR RECKLESS

ENDANGERMENT OF PIGS.

IF APPREHENDED, PLEASE CALL TOLL-FREE

1-800-844-4736.

I handed the notice back to Principal McNutt, who said, "You are obviously the children in these drawings. The children in these drawings are obviously you. Do you have anything to say for your-selves?"

I didn't see any point in denying it. "Only that we would never deliberately endanger a pig," I said.

"Also, we may have entered, but we didn't break anything," Emily Holmes said. "The fence was already broken when we got there."

"Are you going to expel us?" Kevin Applebab asked.

"No, I'm not going to expel you." Principal McNutt combed the thin, white hair back from his forehead. "I don't know exactly what you three did to make Howard Thigpen so mad, but I can tell you that he and his security staff will be searching all the schools in town for you this afternoon. They called here half an hour ago. What I'm going to do, then—wink, wink—is suspend you. Effective immediately. For the rest of the day. I suggest you stay away from video arcades, movie theaters, and bowling alleys—any place where kids usually go. That's where he'll come looking for you when he's done inspecting the schools."

I could tell that Kevin Applebab and Emily

Holmes were as surprised as I was. Why was Principal McNutt trying to help us? It didn't make any sense. We all wanted to ask him and kept making the sort of noises that come at the beginning of sentences, little sounds like "Er—" and "I—," but we couldn't manage to get the words out.

"This will all blow over in a few days," Principal McNutt finished. "I suggest in the meantime that you try to stay out of Howard Thigpen's way. He's not a good man to make an enemy of." He plucked a few of the marbles out of the bowl on his desk and began clacking them together in the palm of his hand. "You kids can escort yourselves off the school grounds," he said. "That will be all." He gestured toward the door.

We stood up from our chairs and were on our way out when I finally worked up the nerve to ask him the question that was on our minds. I couldn't stop myself. "I don't understand. *Why* aren't we in trouble?"

Principal McNutt sighed. "Because of Howard Thigpen. The entire student body watched me sing 'Girls Just Want to Have Fun' by Cyndi Lauper while I stood on one foot," he said. "I'm told that I sounded like a little girl. To be perfectly frank, Mr. Ruggles, *I don't like him.*"

He took the slip of paper with our pictures on it, folded it precisely in half, and let it drop into the trash can. "Dismissed!" he said.

THIRTEEN

In spite of Principal McNutt's warning, we decided to make another trip to the factory complex. The simple truth was that we were the only people who had received the three messages from Ned Hajimura—at least so far as we knew—and he needed our help. Our first step would be to look for him in the potato chip factory. Then, if he wasn't there, we would try to find Room 422.

We walked to the bus stop outside the bagel restaurant and waited for the 12:45 bus. It was right on time, but when we climbed on board and checked our pockets, it turned out that none of us had any quarters. We had spent our last ones at the vending machine yesterday.

The driver made us step back out onto the sidewalk. "Next bus is in half an hour," he said.

We watched him pull away in a cloud of black exhaust.

"Well," Emily Holmes said, "we have until one-fifteen. Does anybody know where we can get some money?"

"I think I do," I said. "Follow me."

My grandfather keeps a glass jug filled with pocket change in the hallway at the top of our staircase. The jug is humongous, packed to the brim with fifty years' worth of quarters, dimes, nickels, and pennies. He always says that he is going to gather the coins into rolls and take them to the bank one day, but he never seems to get around to it.

We made the hike from the bus stop to the antique store in just under ten minutes and found my grandfather having another recycling argument with Shimerman in the front room.

"I say it's nothing but a broken rubber band, and I say it belongs in the trash!" he exclaimed.

"Did you know that the rubber band wasn't invented until eighteen forty-five?" Shimerman said.

"When I throw something away, by God, I expect it to *stay* thrown away!"

"Paper boys used to have to tie their newspapers together with string. Slingshots were made out of horsehair and leather."

"How would you like it if *I* went digging through *your* trash? Well? How would you like *that*, Shimerman?"

"Imagine, a world without rubber bands," Shimerman said, shaking his head.

This was how their arguments went when neither of them was really all that interested.

I told my grandfather that we had come home to borrow some money for a trip we were going to take that afternoon, and he waved us upstairs. I didn't specifically say that the money was for a school field trip, but that's probably what he thought I meant. My grandfather and I both took coins from the change jug all the time, but we tossed our pocket money back in every night before we went to bed, and the pile of coins inside the jug never seemed to fall too far below the rim. Kevin Applebab and Emily Holmes and I fished a few dollars in quarters out of the jug and headed back to the bus stop.

The Factory Row bus pulled up just a minute or two after we got there, and we paid the fare and took our seats. We were still a little sore from the battering the pigs had given us the day before, and we sat up front so that we wouldn't feel the bumps in the road.

"It's lucky my grandfather didn't see the poster with our pictures on it," I said. "He probably would have grounded me, or at least told me to stay away from Howard Thigpen. There's no way we could rescue Ned Hajimura if I was stuck at home all day."

"My parents didn't see the poster either," Kevin Applebab said, "but I worked out a plan in case they do." Apparently, there was another kid in town who looked just like Kevin Applebab—the same tall, lanky body, the same peach-pit-sized Adam's apple, the same muddy brown eyeglasses—except that he had a bigger nose. "My parents and I have spotted him twice now in the grocery store, and then once in a hamburger place, and then one more time at the North Mellwood Shopping Mall. If they see the poster, I'll just say that the kid in the picture must be my look-alike."

"My mom saw the notice on the news last night," Emily Holmes said. "She asked me whether anybody got hurt, and I said I didn't think so, and then she asked me whether I had thrown a wrench in the works of big business, and I said maybe, and then she said, 'Good for you, honey.' That was it—our whole conversation."

From what she told us about her mom, and from what I already knew about her sister, Cinnamon, it looked like Emily Holmes might be the normal one in the family.

We got off the bus nine or ten blocks away from the Thigpen Corporation Factory Complex, at the same stop where we had caught our ride into North Mellwood the day before. We figured it would be a dumb idea to use a bus stop too close to the front gate. After all, Howard Thigpen was on the lookout for us, and he might have stationed extra security guards there, or trained dogs, or who knew what else.

We cut through a patch of trees and bushes until we reached the stump-covered hillside next to the factories. Then we climbed over the hill toward the gap in the fence. We were careful to make sure nobody could see us from the road, ducking into the grass every time we heard a car driving around the bend. Just as the row of brick-shaped buildings came into sight, the factory bell clanged. We watched a huge crowd of factory workers flow through the doors.

The creek bed was still empty. We wriggled underneath the fence without too much trouble, and pretty soon we were standing right in the middle of the factory workers. Once again, they barely seemed to notice us. Kevin Applebab even tested one of them by stopping directly in front of him and snapping in his face. The guy just wrinkled his brow for a second—as though he thought he might have heard a mosquito, but he wasn't quite sure—and then his eyes went dead again.

"Amazing," Kevin Applebab whispered. "It's like that movie where all the people get taken over by pod creatures from outer space."

"Or that issue of *The Uncanny X-Men* where Professor X gets the flu and ends up accidentally controlling the minds of every mutant in Mutant Manor," I said.

"I love that one," Kevin Applebab said.

The potato chip factory was in building number 2, and we waded through the crowd until we had made our way to the front door. When the bell rang again, we followed a group of factory workers inside, wearing a dazed look on our faces in an effort to blend in.

We began to look for Ned Hajimura. The potato chip factory was almost as busy with machines as the blue jeans factory. We saw a **CRUNCH MACHINE** that was frying batches of potato chips in vegetable oil. We saw a **FLAVOR MACHINE** that was spraying the chips with some sort of juice. We saw a **BAG MACHINE** that was stuffing the chips into Thigpen Brand Potato Chips bags. It took us a while to spot the **RIDGE MACHINE**, which was hidden behind a mound of potatoes on the far side of the room, but when we did, we knew that was where Ned Hajimura would be.

The Ridge Machine reminded me a bit of the Groove Machine in the blue jeans factory. It was made up of a thin row of comblike blades that scraped the ridges into the bottom and top of each potato chip. The blades were rounded at the tip to give the chips a sort of ripply look. Curls of fresh potato fell into a bin at the edge of the machine, where two pigs were greedily eating them. They were the same pigs that had gone missing the day before, I guessed. An extremely large man with a feathery black mustache was controlling the blades. Every so often he would look around to make sure no one was watching him. Then he would hold some sort of miniature microphone up to the blades and lean forward to whisper something into it.

I stood behind him and called out, "Are you Ned Hajimura?"

The extremely large man spun around to look at us. He hid the microphone inside his overalls. "Who are you?" he asked suspiciously.

"We got your message," I said. I pulled the blue jeans out of my backpack. "You know, the blue jeans."

He flailed his arms at me. "Put those away!" he shouted. "Do you want us to get caught!?"

He was nothing like the other factory workers we had met. For one thing, he didn't seem to be out of it in quite the same way—even with all the noise and commotion of the potato chip machines, he was still right there in front of us. For another, he was so jittery that I thought he would fall over if we so much as clapped at him. And then there was his mustache, and his overalls, and his generally oversized appearance.

He turned around so that he was facing the machine again and whispered to us out of the corner of his mouth. "Meet me in the potato chip storage room when the next bell rings. We'll talk there." He shooed us away.

The three of us found the potato chip storage room without too much trouble. It was at the back end of the factory, between a machine that packed the bags of chips into plastic trays and a row of docks where the delivery trucks picked them up. The only light came from the open door. We hid behind a column of plastic trays and kept quiet. We had to wait a long time before the bell rang, but shortly after it did, we saw the immense globe of Ned Hajimura's silhouette standing in the doorway. He looked like I might look if you ran me through a photocopying machine and pressed the ENLARGE × 3 button.

"Are you kids in here?" he whispered.

"Behind the potato chip trays," Emily Holmes said. "Third column on your left."

Ned Hajimura shuffled over. "You're the same

kids from the wanted posters, aren't you?" he said.

"That's us," I told him. "We found your message in the blue jeans and then your message in the potato chips. We came here yesterday to investigate."

"And to frighten some poor innocent pigs?" Ned Hajimura accused.

"That happened at the last minute," Kevin Applebab said. "But listen—there are a lot of things we don't understand. Like what's in Room 422?"

"And what do you mean by, 'He's stealing the light from our eyes'?"

"And how did you get those messages in the blue jeans and potato chips in the first place? It *was* you who put them there, wasn't it?"

It was just light enough for me to see Ned Hajimura nodding. "It was me. I figured out how to do it when I was working the Groove Machine in the blue jeans factory. You see, the needles the machine uses to sew the grooves into the blue jeans are just like the needles you use to cut music into a record album. I used to work at a record factory when I was a teenager, so I know what I'm talking about. All I had to do was find a way to make the needles vibrate along with my voice. That's what I use my microphone for."

He took the microphone out of his overalls and held it up to his lips. The volume knob was turned to the lowest setting. "I place it against the needles, and they record my voice inside the blue jeans. It's the same principle with the Ridge Machine and the potato chips. Sometimes the factory is so loud that it threatens to drown me out, but fortunately my voice is naturally rich and vibrant. Don't you think?"

He cleared his throat and sang "*Mi, mi, mi, mi.*"

We all agreed that his voice was very nice.

"Thank you," he said modestly. "I used to sing in a funk band."

"How did you know that someone would listen to your messages?" Kevin Applebab asked.

"I didn't," Ned Hajimura said. "It's like throwing a bottle into the ocean with a note inside it. You just hope the waves will take it somewhere where someone will find it. But I knew that if I put a real note inside the blue jeans, the factory inspectors would destroy it. Then I would be in even more trouble than I already am. You have to realize, they've been watching me pretty closely since I found out about Room 422. They even make me sleep here at night. I have a bed on the top floor of the tennis shoe factory."

"But you still haven't told us what this Room 422 business is all about," Emily Holmes said.

"Room 422 is where he keeps the machine."

"Who's 'he'? And what machine?"

Ned Hajimura shuddered. "Howard Thigpen. And the Spark Transplantation Machine."

A potato chip bag rustled in the silence of the storage room, and Ned Hajimura nearly jumped out of his clothes. "Run for your lives!" he shouted.

Ned stuffed the microphone back into his overalls and bolted for the door. Then he realized it was just Kevin Applebab leaning against one of the potato chip trays with his elbow. "What, are you trying to give me a heart attack?" he said.

He took a few deep breaths, turned around, and stooped back down beside us. His voice fell to a whisper. "Anyway, I thought Room 422 was just a rumor at first. But then the other factory workers began to join Howard Thigpen for what he called 'meetings.' They came out acting like zombies. Some of them were my friends, and they didn't even seem to remember me. It was like all the personality had been sucked right out of them. *You've seen them. You* know what they're like. So I did some snooping around, and what I discovered was horrible."

Just then the factory bell rang, and a moment later we heard the rolling-thunder sound of hundreds of footsteps as the factory workers marched back to their machines.

Ned Hajimura tugged nervously at his overalls. "We're out of time," he said. "If I'm not back at the Ridge Machine in sixty seconds, they'll come looking for me. Look, you kids have to disable the Spark Transplantation Machine. It's the only way. I would do it myself, but they would spot me coming from a mile away."

He hurried to the door, moving in a sort of breakneck waddle, but stopped on his way out.

"*Room 422,*" he repeated. "It's in building number 4, the shaving cream factory."

Then he was gone.

Emily Holmes, Kevin Applebab, and I didn't

even know what a Spark Transplantation Machine was, much less how to go about disabling one. But we decided that the best thing to do would be to find Room 422 and figure out what to do from there.

We left the potato chip factory by the back door, climbing down from the loading docks into an alley paved with cracked gray asphalt. We could see a parking lot on the other side of the chain-link fence. It was filled with cars shining like puddles of wet paint. There were a few trucks idling in the alley, and factory workers were loading them up with boxes of blue jeans and toothbrushes and tennis shoes. As usual, the factory workers didn't seem to notice us, but it didn't take long for one of the truck drivers to spot us. "Excuse me," he said, leaning out his window, "but what are you children doing here?"

We took off running. We sprinted past the five factory buildings that were between us and the empty creek bed and shot underneath the fence. When we heard feet tramping after us, we hid in the tall grass, lying flat on our stomachs. A dozen security guards rushed around the corner of the factory, looking this way and that. They couldn't seem to figure out where we had gone.

"Check inside the Dumpster!" one of them ordered.

"Did they climb up the side of the factory?"

"Look under that rock!"

Finally, they began to drift away from our hiding place, checking behind doorways and gutters and along the front side of the building for us.

When they were out of hearing range, Emily Holmes whispered, "What do we do now? How on earth do we sneak back inside?"

I shook my head.

"We don't," I said. "At least not this afternoon. We'll have to try again tomorrow."

FOURTEEN

Things were different in the school courtyard the next morning, although it took me a while to put my finger on it.

The kids who usually just ignored me—and the other kids, the ones who usually wobbled their bellies and said "ruggles, ruggles, ruggles" whenever I walked by—got really quiet when they saw me. They pointed and watched me pass. I could hear them whispering to one another. One kid even spilled his folders onto the ground when he saw me and didn't pick them up until the wind had blown his papers all over the place.

Eventually, a ninth grader I recognized as one of the star players on the football team stopped me in the hall and asked, "Are you that kid who massacred all the pigs?"

"First of all," I told him, "it wasn't me. And

second of all, I didn't massacre them, I just got on their nerves a little."

The ninth grader walked away looking confused.

I saw Kevin Applebab and Emily Holmes a few minutes later and asked them about all of this. They said that the same sort of thing had been happening to them.

"They've even stopped calling me Rash Butt," Kevin said.

It turned out that most of the kids in school had seen the wanted poster with our pictures on it, and the ones who hadn't seen it personally had at least heard about it from the other kids. Some of them were under the impression that the three of us had killed dozens of pigs with our bare hands, and some of them believed that the pigs had killed *us*. Some of them thought that the whole thing was a hoax or a publicity stunt cooked up by the Thigpen Corporation to sell pigpens. A few of them had seen Howard Thigpen walking through the school building yesterday, and they wanted to know whether he was still after us.

Everybody was still talking about it at the

beginning of Mr. Fred's science class. The whole time he was taking roll I heard people whispering things like, "I thought Howard Thigpen had arrested them," and, "Wait a minute—Dwayne *Ruggles* is the kid from the news?" One kid pretended he was a pro wrestling announcer: "Three lone seventh graders against a hundred pigs! And let me tell you, Jim, the pigs do not like what they see here today! I think we're in for a fight to the finish!"

Finally Mr. Fred had to make an announcement to quiet everybody down: "I realize that we have a celebrity in our midst," he said, "but we do have work to do today. If Howard Thigpen has a problem with Dwayne Ruggles, I'm sure the two of them can work it out between themselves."

The whispering slowly came to a stop, and Mr. Fred spent the rest of the hour teaching us about fingerprints.

"You've probably heard that every person's fingerprints are absolutely unique," he began. "Well, as far as we know, that's true. Scientists say the same thing about snowflakes—that every one is unique—and as far as we know, that's true, too. Of course, nobody has tested every single fingerprint or every single snowflake to find out for sure, but the number of possible snowflake and fingerprint patterns is much, much bigger than the number of actual snowflakes and fingerprints in the world, so it's a pretty safe bet."

He told us about how the skin cells on the tips of our fingers join together to make all sorts of loops and streaks and swirls. Our fingerprints are the same from the day we're born until the day we die, he said, which is why police departments keep the fingerprints of criminals on file: it helps the detectives catch them when they do something wrong. The patterns on the balls of the toes are also unique, he said, although police departments don't keep anyone's toeprints on file.

The whole thing made me think of the Sherlock Holmes movies my grandfather is always watching with Shimerman. I could remember one movie in particular where Sherlock Holmes solved a crime by finding a fingerprint on the face of a watch. I pressed my thumb to the face of my own watch and tried to make out the mark. The light was no good, though, and I couldn't see it. It occurred to me that I had probably left my finger-prints all over the Thigpen Factories. Fortunately I had never broken the law before, so they wouldn't be on file anywhere.

Mr. Fred spent a good fifteen minutes teaching us the way to make a really sharp set of finger-prints. The trick was to sort of *roll* your fingers through the ink—not just press them down flat and lift them right back up, but rotate them until the whole fingertip was covered. After that, you were supposed to turn them over on the piece of paper you were using, one finger at a time. Mr. Fred warned us to be careful not to smudge the prints with our knuckles. Then he handed out a bunch of ink pads, the kind that teachers use with rubber stamps that say things like GOOD JOB! or PLEASE SEE ME AFTER CLASS. We spent the rest of the period making sets of fingerprints on our worksheets.

I had never seen the pattern of my fingerprints so clearly before. It was interesting, the way the grooves swirled and dipped and looped around. They looked like the rainbows of oil you see on top of a puddle. Sometimes the loops would close together in the shape of ovals or teardrops, and sometimes they would come within a hair or two of closing and then shoot off in completely different directions. It was pretty neat.

When we were done, Mr. Fred gave everybody a few sheets of Kleenex and let us wipe the ink from our fingers. I rubbed mine pretty hard, but they were still kind of blue by the time the bell rang.

"Fact for the day," Mr. Fred said as we left: "The only animal in the world with fingerprints that are indistinguishable from a human being's is the koala bear. Oh, and don't forget I want to know what you're planning to do for your science fair projects on Monday. A paragraph or two will be plenty. You have three days to figure it out."

I had been so busy trying to solve the mystery of the blue jeans and potato chips that I had completely forgotten about my science fair project. I promised myself that I would try to come up with something over the weekend.

Meanwhile, I had the rest of the day to get through. And it was quite a day. The people in my second and third period classes were whispering the same sorts of things about me that the kids in Mr. Fred's class had whispered:

"I bet you he made the whole story up just to get attention."

"I heard he showed up today on a motorcycle."

"You know what I blame? I blame peer pressure."

For a seventh grader, I was almost famous.

Even Coach Channering seemed to know who I was for once, although I wasn't sure whether this was a good thing or a bad thing. I mean, he wasn't exactly impressed by me, but he did call me by an insulting nickname—Short Round. Kevin Applebab reminded me later that Short Round was the name of the kid in one of the Indiana Jones movies, but I don't think that was who Coach Channering had in mind.

Every time I heard someone whispering my name, I found myself turning around to see who it was. I couldn't help it. I kept expecting Howard Thigpen to show up with a pack of hired goons to haul me out of school and rough me up, but it never happened.

Maybe Principal McNutt was right. Maybe

Howard Thigpen had found the missing pigs or gotten mad at some other group of children and the commotion had just blown over. Or maybe he only wanted us to *think* it had blown over so that he could set some sort of trap for us. I didn't know.

FIFTEEN

That afternoon, just a few minutes before school ended, the sky turned gray, the shadows disappeared, and it began to pour down rain. Kevin Applebab and Emily Holmes and I found one another in the hallway after the final bell rang. A big group of kids had gathered by the front doors to wait for a break in the storm, and we waited with them. The three of us made plans to meet by the bagel restaurant in time to catch the four thirty bus to the factory complex. We promised one another that we would do whatever it took to find Room 422; after all, Ned Hajimura was counting on us. In the meantime, we would all go home to get our umbrellas and make the appropriate excuses to our families. I would tell my grandfather that Kevin and I were going to see a movie together, and Kevin would tell his parents the same thing.

As for Emily Holmes, I imagined that her

conversation with her mother would go something like this:

EMILY: I'm off to throw another wrench in the works of big business, Mom.

EMILY'S MOM: Okay. See you later, honey.

Then Emily would walk out the door twirling her umbrella and eating a sesame seed bagel.

That's how I pictured it, anyway.

I was soaking wet by the time I got home. I climbed straight upstairs to my bedroom to change clothes, and then I took my umbrella out of my closet and went looking for my grandfather. I came across my umbrella a few years ago in the antique store. It has a long, cane-shaped handle, and the canopy is decorated with a picture of Ms. Pac-Man racing through a maze. You can find some real treasures in the antique store if you look hard enough.

It turned out that I did not have to tell my grandfather I was going to a movie with Kevin Applebab after all, because he had fallen asleep in a chair. My grandfather sometimes has trouble sleeping at night, which is something that happens to a lot of old people. As a result, he occasionally dozes off during the day. I have noticed that this is particularly likely to happen when it rains. It's the sort of thing I've gotten used to.

Shimerman was working at the front counter. On my way out the door I told him to let my grandfather know that I would be back later that night. He said, "You can count on me, Young Ruggles." I don't know why Shimerman began calling me Young Ruggles in the first place, but it had been that way for as long as I could remember. However it began, the name had certainly stuck. He tried calling my grandfather Old Ruggles once or twice, but my grandfather had threatened to cut Shimerman's beard off and glue it to his forehead, which had put a stop to that idea real fast.

Emily Holmes and Kevin Applebab were already waiting for me by the time I got to the bus stop. Kevin Applebab was carrying his purple-and-blue camouflage umbrella, and Emily Holmes had an umbrella with a picture of frogs falling from the sky on it. They were both pretty good umbrellas, but if we had an umbrella contest, mine would definitely win, I thought. We counted our money to make sure we had enough for the bus ride. Between us we had eight dollars and eighty-four cents, and our bus fare would be fifty cents each. That left seven dollars and thirty-four cents, which was plenty.

We rode the bus until we saw the Mellwood Reservoir through the window, and then we got out and walked the rest of the way to the Thigpen Corporation Factory Complex. Everything looked different in the rain. The trees were a darker shade of green, and the grass on the hill was weighed down flat with water. There were lamps we hadn't noticed before on the sides of the factory buildings, sending cones of white light down over the doors and the air vents.

We were planning to get through the chain-link fence the same way we had gotten through the day before—by using the creek bed to slide underneath—but there was one thing we hadn't counted on. When we got to the gap in the fence, we discovered that the gully was flooded with muddy brown water from all the rain. The water reached as high as the third or fourth link on the fence. Emily Holmes dropped a stick into the stream to see how fast it was going, and the stick vanished right away. We knew there was no way we would be able to squeeze underneath the fence with all that water in the way.

"We could try climbing over," Kevin Applebab suggested. "Maybe it isn't as hard as it looks."

"Or what if we sawed through a few of the links? Maybe we could get in like that," I said. But as soon as I mentioned it I realized that I didn't have anything with me that would be good for sawing. My house key might work, but it would take me a million years to saw through a fence with a house key. I wished that I had brought my Swiss army knife with me.

"The obvious thing to do," Emily Holmes said, "is hide out inside one of the delivery trucks and sneak through like that. Did anybody see where they drove in?"

"I think I remember seeing a gate on the back side of the potato chip factory," Kevin Applebab said.

"Then that's where we should go," Emily Holmes said.

The three of us began walking along the fence line. After the hill leveled off, we cut through a patch of baby pine trees that were still young enough for us to bend the trunks out of the way.

Then we slogged through a field of mud that almost sucked the shoes from my feet. Even though I was carrying my umbrella, I was still soaking wet, and I thought about how nice it would be to stand beneath one of those automatic hot-air dryers you find in public restrooms. When we came to the parking lot, we ducked down behind the bumpers of the cars so that we couldn't be seen from the factories. It didn't take long for us to find the gate Kevin Applebab had seen the day before. Unfortunately, it was closed. There was a complicated-looking lock on it, about the size of a pumpkin. A sign bolted to the gate said—

NOTICE
THE THIGPEN CORPORATION FACTORY COMPLEX
ADMITS DELIVERY TRUCKS
ONLY BETWEEN THE HOURS OF TEN AND FOUR.
ALL UNSCHEDULED DELIVERY TRUCKS
SHOULD RETURN AT THESE DESIGNATED TIMES.

It was Friday evening. There were no trucks in sight.

We stood behind a minivan for a few minutes

listening to the rain patter against our umbrellas and trying to work out a new plan. I was hoping that Emily Holmes would have another idea as good as her one about the delivery truck, but she didn't. Neither did Kevin Applebab, and neither did I.

In the end, we decided that the only thing we could do was keep circling around the chain-link fence looking for another way in. We walked past the rest of the potato chip factory and then past the tennis shoe factory, and then we turned around the corner. We were now on the side of the building that bordered the Mellwood Reservoir, and we could see drops of rain bouncing up from the water like popcorn. Unfortunately, we couldn't find any more gaps in the fence. It was still too tall for us to climb—plus the metal links were more slippery than ever now that they were wet. Eventually, we ended up exactly where we had started a couple of days before, by the swinging iron gate and the security booth in front of the factories. We were completely out of options.

"Well, guys, it looks like this is our only way in," I said. "We'll have to give it a try. But be ready to run if you hear anybody coming."

It had gotten darker as we walked around the buildings, and a silvery light was shining from the window of the security booth. Rain sparkled as it fell into the light and then winked out again as it reached the other side. The window was so foggy that I couldn't make out anything more than a shadow behind it, but I knocked on it anyway.

The first thing I saw when the window opened was an enormous gray beard. "Well, well, well," the beard said. "If it isn't my good buddy Clarence."

Then a face appeared behind all the hair. It was Earl the security guard.

"Like I told you, you're not getting in without ID cards," he said.

"Come on, Earl, my man. What if we make it worth your while?" I asked.

He rolled his eyes at me. "What could you possibly have that would 'make it worth my while'? You're just a strange little kid with a Ms. Pac-Man umbrella."

Kevin Applebab and Emily Holmes were hovering just over my shoulder. "We can give you seven dollars and thirty-four cents," I said.

Earl the security guard laughed. "Seven dollars

and thirty-four cents? I should call Howard Thigpen on you right now. You *are* those kids he's looking for, *aren't* you?" He tapped the wanted poster that was tacked to the wall behind him.

I felt sick to my stomach. "Look, what will it take to get you to let us through the gate?" I said.

"There's only one thing in the world I want, and you can't get it for me."

"Name it."

He shrugged. "Whatever you say, 'Clarence.' My hobby is Internet auction sites. I sell American cultural memorabilia to collectors from Japan—lunch boxes, posters, record albums, things like that. There's one American record that's the hottest Japanese collector's item in the world right now. I could make a bundle if I could get my hands on it, but I haven't been able to find it anywhere. The only thing I want—and there's no way you can get it for me—is one hundred copies of 'Ghostbusters' by Ray Parker Jr."

I looked at Kevin Applebab and Emily Holmes. They were both smiling.

"I think that might be something we can work out," I said.

SIXTEEN

Gadzooks—North Mellwood's biggest comic book store—was getting ready to close down for the night when we got there. The owner had already turned the lights off, and he was flipping the sign in the window over from the side that showed a picture of Dr. Doom saying COME IN—IF YOU DARE! to the side that showed a picture of the Thing saying IT'S CLOSIN' TIME! Both the Thing and Dr. Doom appear in a comic book called *The Fantastic Four*. The Thing is basically a big orange pile of rocks who fights crime and complains about how ugly he is all the time. Dr. Doom is one of his archenemies—a madman in an iron mask who tries to take over the world and complains about how ugly *he* is all the time.

The Fantastic Four is not one of my favorites.

When the comic book store owner saw us standing outside, he cracked the door open and said, "We're shutting down. You guys will have to come back tomorrow."

I told him, "We're looking for Mr. Fred."

"Fred Boosey?" he asked. "Short guy? Shaped kind of like half a hot dog? He lives upstairs." He pointed to a door that was right next to his own.

"Thanks," we told him, and he said, "Don't mention it. Just buy lots of comic books."

Mr. Fred lived at the top of a long, narrow flight of stairs. There was only one door there, a tall red one with a mail slot at the bottom and a big brass knob in the center. When we knocked on it, we heard his voice calling, "Just a minute! It's twelve dollars and seventy-two cents, right?"

He undid the lock and opened the door. He looked surprised to see us. "Dwayne Ruggles!" he said. "Kevin Applebab! Emily Holmes! I thought you guys were my pizza arriving. To what do I owe the pleasure?"

"We have a favor to ask you," Emily Holmes said. "We wouldn't have come by your house, except that it's an emergency."

Mr. Fred nodded. "I understand. Please come in."

There was an umbrella stand by the door, and we shook the rain from our umbrellas, folded them, and put them inside. Mr. Fred led us into his living room, where we took a seat on the couch behind his coffee table. These were basically the only two normal pieces of furniture in the entire room—the couch and the coffee table. The rest of the furniture was all columns of record albums in cardboard sleeves. Some of the columns were only as high as our knees, but some of them reached almost to the ceiling. At first I didn't see the TV anywhere, but eventually I spotted it on top of one of the columns. It was roughly the size of a toaster—the smallest TV I had ever seen. On the walls were hundreds of comic books in clear Mylar bags. I spotted the entire *Punisher* miniseries and the first ten issues of *Fizz and the Amazing Plop* and the hard-to-find issue of *Batman* where Robin gets eaten by a flock of angry chickens. Mr. Fred even had *Giant-Size X-Men* #1, which marks the first appearance of Colossus, Storm, and Nightcrawler and is worth even more than the regular *X-Men* #1.

The column of record albums directly next to

the couch had a table lamp on top of it. Mr. Fred switched it on. "So tell me about this emergency of yours," he said.

"It's kind of a long story," Kevin Applebab answered. "It has to do with Howard Thigpen. I'm sure you heard he's looking for us. That's because we sneaked into his factories and ran off some of his pigs. The pig part was an accident, but we found out that something terrible is going on there—"

"Only we don't quite know what," Emily Holmes interrupted.

"That's right," Kevin Applebab said. "We don't quite know what. But it has something to do with a Spark Transplantation Machine, and there's this guy named Ned Hajimura who needs our help and—"

I took up where he left off. "And we have to get back into the factories, but we're having trouble because it's raining, and Earl the security guard won't let us through the front gate."

"But why do you need *my* help?" Mr. Fred asked.

I took a deep breath.

"We need one hundred copies of 'Ghostbusters' by Ray Parker Jr.," I said.

"Are you kidding?" Mr. Fred asked. I could hear the excitement rising in his voice. "*Of course* you can have one hundred copies of 'Ghostbusters' by Ray Parker Jr.! Heck, you can have two hundred copies!" He leaped up from the couch and took a plant down from one of the record album stacks. "There are probably five hundred of them in this stack alone!"

"Maybe we *could* take a few extra," Emily Holmes said. "Just to be on the safe side."

"Take as many as you want," Mr. Fred insisted. "They're like a plague of locusts to me."

We were helping Mr. Fred count the "Ghostbusters" records when there was a knock at the door. It was the pizza delivery boy. Mr. Fred gave him fifteen dollars and came back in carrying two large pizzas. "It's amazing," he said. "With the specials they run these days, it's cheaper to get two large pizzas with everything than one medium pizza with pineapple and black olives, which is what I really wanted. Would you kids like to eat dinner with me?"

The pizzas smelled really good, and none of us had eaten anything since lunch. We had done an awful lot of hiking and bus riding since then, so we had worked up quite an appetite. We agreed to eat with Mr. Fred. The four of us sat around the coffee table taking pizza slices right out of the box and drinking cans of root beer and Sprite and orange soda. Mr. Fred also had some of that King Bubble stuff we had seen in the vending machines inside the office building. I tried a sip of the sweet green tea flavor, but it was too weird for me—spicy and tangy, but sort of salty and bitter at the same time. I want to say that it tasted like grass, but maybe that's just because it was green.

In the end, after we helped Mr. Fred finish off the pizzas, we decided to take one hundred and fifty copies of "Ghostbusters" with us. The hardest part was figuring out how to carry them all. They were heavy and oddly shaped. Even with just fifty records apiece, we knew that it would be a struggle to get them all downstairs, much less all the way to the Thigpen Factories. Eventually, Mr. Fred found a box that would fit all one hundred and fifty of the records, wrapped a plastic trash bag around the box to keep it dry, and helped us tug it down from his apartment. The box bumped noisily from step to step. It was packed so tightly, though, that I didn't think any of the records would break.

"There's always more where these came from," Mr. Fred told us when we were standing in front of the comic book store. "All you have to do is ask."

"One hundred and fifty should be plenty," I said. "But thanks, Mr. Fred."

"Yeah, thanks," said Emily Holmes and Kevin Applebab.

Mr. Fred went back inside.

We managed to get the box of "Ghostbusters" records to the bus stop by dragging it along the sidewalk most of the way, but we had to pick it up every time we crossed the street, hurrying across like a giant crab. Emily Holmes and I would take the two front corners, and Kevin Applebab, because his arms were longer, would take the back two. "This is nothing but height discrimination," he complained, but we couldn't think of any other way to do it.

We were completely exhausted by the time we got to the bus stop, not to mention dripping wet.

We had discovered pretty quickly that we couldn't hold our umbrellas open and haul the box at the same time, so we had put the umbrellas away and simply trudged through the rain. It had slacked off a little since that afternoon, but it was still falling hard enough to leave us totally drenched.

As we waited for the bus to arrive, we talked about what we would have to do when we got back to the Thigpen Factories. Unless we ran into some sort of trouble, we figured there would be three steps:

Step one: Get through the front gate by giving the "Ghostbusters" records to Earl the security guard.

Step two: Find Room 422.

Step three: Break the Spark Transplantation Machine—whatever that was.

I didn't know about Emily Holmes and Kevin Applebab, but I was much more worried about step three than I was about steps one and two. What exactly *was* a Spark Transplantation Machine, I wondered? How big was it? Would it be hard to break? What if it was booby-trapped with poisoned darts or electricity or something? I couldn't imagine it would be as easy as finding a sign that said PUSH THIS BUTTON TO BREAK MACHINE, no matter *how* organized Howard Thigpen was.

We must have waited at the bus stop by the bagel restaurant for a good half hour before we realized that the bus wasn't coming. The final departure time, according to the sign on the pole, was exactly 8:45. We had missed it by ten minutes.

SEVENTEEN

The Thigpen Corporation Factory Complex was too far away for us to make the trip on foot. It would have been too far away even *without* a box full of "Ghostbusters" records to deal with, but *with* them—and in the rain—we knew we would never make it. We decided to leave the records in my grandfather's antique store overnight and set out for the factories first thing in the morning.

The next day, when I woke up, I told my grandfather that I was going to spend the night with Kevin Applebab. Meanwhile, Kevin Applebab told his parents that he was going to spend the night with me. I had heard about this particular trick years ago, but this was the first time I had tried it myself. It was supposed to be foolproof, and if it worked, we could stay out as late as we wanted.

I made sure the Thigpen Brand Blue Jeans and the Victrola horn were in my backpack, and then I waited for Kevin Applebab and Emily Holmes to show up to help me carry the "Ghostbusters" records. We ended up leaving fifty of them in the antique store, hiding them behind a tepee of broken water skis so that none of the customers would find them. We figured the fifty extra records would give us leverage in case we had problems with Earl the security guard. We weren't really sure we could trust him.

As it turned out, we had nothing to worry about. Earl was still on duty when the bus dropped us off in front of the factories. Or maybe he was back on duty, I didn't know for sure. In either case, he was there waiting for us. A new shift must have been starting, because we had to stand in line behind a crowd of factory workers before we finally reached the security booth. The rain had stopped, but there were still puddles everywhere we looked. The workers seemed to shuffle through them without even noticing they were there. Their shoes turned dark as they soaked up the water.

"So, the Odd Squad returns," Earl said when we reached the window. "What took you kids so long?"

"We had bus trouble," I said, "but we finally made it."

"I can see that *you* made it," Earl said, "but what about the 'Ghostbusters' records?"

Kevin Applebab, Emily Holmes, and I hoisted the box we had carried onto the ledge of the window. It was pretty mangled by this point, and Earl squinted doubtfully at it. When he opened it up and pulled out a handful of records, though, he couldn't keep himself from shouting. "Great Mother of Moses!" he said. "'Ghostbusters' records! The real deal!"

"We lived up to our end of the bargain, now you have to live up to yours," I said. "Let us through the gate."

"And they're still in the original cellophane!" Earl said. "The Japanese love things that are still in their original cellophane! It triples the value!"

"There are more where these came from if you don't double-cross us, amigo," I said.

For some reason, Earl thought this was funny. He pressed a button and the gate wheeled open and he waved us through. As we walked into the courtyard, I heard him saying "double-cross" to himself, and then "amigo." He gave his leg a meaty slap. "Okay, Philip Marlowe," he said. "Okay, Dick Tracy." His voice faded away as the gate closed behind us.

We followed a few of the workers to building number 4, the shaving cream factory. They were all wearing hard hats and aprons. The aprons were covered with faded blue shaving cream. Kevin Applebab, Emily Holmes, and I were just wearing our regular shirts and blue jeans, but we did our best to blend in anyway. We pretended we were factory workers. We slouched our shoulders and sort of drifted along without talking or noticing anything. I found that it helped if I imagined I was just a pair of Thigpen Brand Tennis Shoes sliding along a conveyor belt.

When we got to the shaving cream factory, the workers ran their ID cards through a laser scanner that clocked them in. Then they made their way to their machines. Kevin Applebab, Emily Holmes, and I ducked to the side. We crept along the wall until we were hidden behind a big, rumbling vat of blue-green shaving goo. The smell of peppermint washed over us.

"Where do you think Room 422 is?" Kevin Applebab asked.

The shaving cream factory wasn't as loud as the blue jeans or potato chips factories had been, but it was still pretty noisy, and he had to lift his voice so that we would hear him.

I looked out over the floor of the factory. All I could see were the various machines stirring and pumping and bottling the shaving cream. It was pretty obvious that none of *them* was Room 422. Maybe Room 422 was concealed behind a fake wall or a trapdoor, I thought. Or maybe it wasn't a room at all—maybe it was right here on the factory floor, and Howard Thigpen just *called* it "Room 422" in order to throw people off the scent.

"I bet it's up there," said Emily Holmes. She was motioning to a staircase I hadn't noticed before. At the top of the staircase was a platform that forked off into two hallways. A sign hanging between the hallways said—

ROOMS 400–413—THIS WAY →

←THAT WAY—ROOMS 414–425

"Just a wild guess," said Emily.

The three of us worked our way across the room, looked around to make sure no one was watching, and rushed to the top of the stairs. We could see the entire factory from up there: the workers in aprons and hard hats, the long row of machines, and the doors that led, on one side, to the pigpen factory and, on the other, to the blue jeans factory.

We followed the arrow that pointed to Room 422. The hallway twisted and turned for a while before veering away to the left. Gradually, the noise of the machines faded to a sort of low rumble with an occasional ticking sound inside of it. I guessed that we were somewhere over the shaving cream factory by now. Room 422 was at the end of the hall. I had been worried that there might be security guards there, but I didn't see any. Still, we decided it was best to be careful.

We walked the last few yards to the room very slowly. The door looked like just a normal wooden door, the kind of door you'd see in any office building, with a black plate that had the number 422 stamped on it in white letters. I was kind of disappointed. I could see that Emily Holmes and Kevin Applebab were thinking the same thing. We had been expecting something more dramatic, I guess—a giant golden gate, maybe, or a huge steel bank vault–type door with a wheel-shaped lock on it.

I put my hand on the doorknob. "Should we try it?" I asked. I didn't wait for Emily Holmes and Kevin Applebab to answer. I gave the knob a twist, and it turned beneath my palm. The door was unlocked. I pushed it open, and we stepped inside.

The room seemed just like a normal office room, mostly. The carpet was the kind that is hard and flat beneath your feet—good for racing Hot Wheels on, but not so good for taking naps on. It smelled slightly of glue. There was a coffeepot on top of a filing cabinet in the corner. Someone had left the overhead fluorescent lights running, and the room was quiet enough for us to hear them buzzing in the air. In fact, the only thing out of the ordinary about the place was the Spark Transplantation Machine.

The Spark Transplantation Machine was a metal box with a plunger attached to the top. It looked like one of the detonators that miners use to set off dynamite. On either side of the metal box was a big clear glass bell connected to the box by a thick cord and to the other bell by a clear rubber hose. One of the bells was about the size of a refrigerator, and the other was about the size of a bathroom or a walk-in closet. They reminded me of The Cone of Silence on the old TV show *Get Smart*, if you've ever seen that before. Inside each of the bells was a chair. The chair in the larger bell had metal shackles fastened to it.

It was strange to see such a peculiar-looking device in the middle of an ordinary office room. We could tell it was the Spark Transplantation Machine because of the sign that was bolted to it. The sign read: **SPARK TRANSPLANTATION MACHINE**.

"Well, it looks like we found it," Kevin Applebab said. "What's next?"

"Step Three," I said. "Break Spark Transplantation Machine."

"But how on earth do we do that?"

"You don't," said a voice. The voice came from the doorway behind us.

We turned around. It was Howard Thigpen.

"I thought you three might show up eventually," he said. "I can see that I was right. Sometimes all you have to do is sit back and wait, and the very thing you're looking for will fall right into your lap. Just one of the many lessons of business."

Howard Thigpen was not a particularly big man, and I was pretty sure the three of us could knock him down and make our escape if we tried. Before we got the chance, though, the gigantic shape of Ned Hajimura moved into the doorway. My heart gave a leap! Howard Thigpen did not seem to notice him.

I figured Ned was coming to save us. I imagined him grabbing Howard Thigpen around the chest, pinning his arms to his sides, and telling us to run for our lives. But then I saw the look in his eyes.

They were dull and empty, as gray as the inside of a well.

Also, for some reason, his mustache was missing.

"Mr. Hajimura," Howard Thigpen told him, "please subdue these children."

EIGHTEEN

Ned Hajimura captured us without too much trouble. We tried to shove our way past him, but it was no use. Trying to push him out of the way was like trying to topple over a hill—that's how big he was. "Take them across the hall to Room 423," Howard Thigpen told him, and Ned Hajimura carried us like we were nothing but blocks of wood, with me under one arm (because I was heavier, I guessed) and Kevin Applebab and Emily Holmes under the other. We squirmed and struggled, but he didn't pay any attention to us.

Room 423 was like Room 422 without the Spark Transplantation Machine—a normal office room with a desk, a lamp, and a filing cabinet. Ned Hajimura stood us up against the back wall of the room and lumbered out of the way. Then Howard Thigpen came in and began his interrogation.

"Now then," he said. "Suppose you children

tell me what you know."

I decided to play a hunch. "We know absolutely everything."

Howard Thigpen stared me in the eyes. "You're lying."

"No, we're not," I told him. "We know about the Spark Transplantation Machine, and Room 422, and your 'meetings' with the factory workers."

"And the rhinestones," added Emily Holmes. "Don't forget the rhinestones."

"That's right. We know about the rhinestones, too."

It was obvious that this last part—the part about the rhinestones—had really gotten to him. His entire face seemed to pucker as he tried to decide whether we were telling the truth. The lights in his shadow became very bright all of a sudden, twitching and quivering like stars reflected in the surface of a lake. Eventually he made a clicking sound with his tongue—it was the same sound my grandfather always makes when Shimerman starts talking about the dangers of Styrofoam—and slowly shook his head. He gave a big, catlike smile.

"You're lying," he said. "You don't know anything. But I'm going to tell you."

And with that he began pacing around the room, walking until he reached one of the walls and then swinging around to walk the other way. He reminded me of a pinball.

This is what he said to us: "The best thing about having money, children, isn't what you can buy with it. You can buy many things, of course. Mansions and motorcycles. Fruit pies and sailboats. Parking garages and junior high schools. But anybody who has lots of money to spend will tell you that these things can only keep you entertained for so long. No, the best thing about having money is *making other people do what you want*. You can make people paint themselves with zebra stripes. You can make people pretend they're spinning a hula hoop. You can make people stand all day staring at blue jeans or toothbrushes or potato chips.

"You can make people do almost anything. But you can't make them respect you. You can make them *pretend* to respect you, but you can't make them *really* respect you.

"The more money I made, the more obvious this became to me," Howard Thigpen said. "I could buy power. I could buy happiness. But I couldn't buy respect. I searched in vain for a solution.

"It was five years ago, shortly before I moved to North Mellwood, that I found one. It was then that I began wearing my rhinestone jacket. I bought it on a whim. Not only did it make me look slim and handsome—as anyone can tell you a rhinestone jacket will do—but people paid more attention to me when I wore it. They looked at me when I passed on the street. They listened when I spoke. They said things like, 'You certainly look fancy today,' and 'I could see you coming from a mile away, Mr. Thigpen.'

"In short, they *respected* me. But why? What had changed? I realized that it could only be one thing—the dazzle of the rhinestones. I called it 'the rhinestone effect.'

"I determined that this 'rhinestone effect' would only grow stronger with the addition of more rhinestones to my jacket. So I began having them added at The Ritzy Button, North

Mellwood's premier men's clothing store. And indeed, the more rhinestones I wore, the more powerful the rhinestone effect grew. Everywhere I went, people stared at me. They couldn't help it. Then, for reasons I will not discuss, my jacket was taken from me. '*Evidence*,' the police called it. But even after my trial was over and I had paid the necessary fines, they did not return it to me. The police chief retired and left the country. I have since received reports that he is living in South America, wearing my rhinestone jacket as he scours the beaches of Brazil and Peru for bottle caps to add to his bottle cap collection. I am sure he is greatly respected.

"For some time after the loss of my rhinestone jacket, I was heartbroken. I bought a new one, of course, but it just wasn't the same. I tried wearing other sorts of fashionable clothing—Hawaiian shirts, smoking jackets, ponchos with pictures of Elvis on them. Nothing worked. I had lost the respect I had earned. Then one day I made a discovery. I was watching some of my factory workers as they talked during a break. One of them told a joke—not a very funny joke—and the others laughed. The joke was, 'Why did the pig cross the road?' and the answer was, 'He was tied to the chicken.'

"As I said, not a particularly funny joke. Anybody who knows the slightest thing about pigs realizes that a pig would never in a million years permit himself to be tied to a chicken. Nonetheless, the other factory workers laughed. And *why*? Because they *respected* the man who had told the joke. I noticed the light shining from his eyes as he basked in their laughter, glimmering like a pair of sparks. I had never looked so carefully into someone else's eyes before, and I was astonished.

"Soon I began to see this light everywhere. Movie stars on talk shows, children with their mothers, lovers in restaurants—they all had these sparks in their eyes, and the brighter the sparks became, the more people seemed to respect them.

"After much observation, I determined that the sparks in their eyes gave rise to—*they were the cause of*—the respect. I thought of the sparks as nature's rhinestones. If only I could *wear* them, I thought, like the rhinestones I had worn on my jacket. Why, the respect I inspired would be endless!

"So I invented the Spark Transplantation Machine. It took me a year of effort, working with the top geniuses in North Mellwood, but eventually I created a machine that did exactly what I wanted it to do. It could take the light out of a person's eyes and transfer it directly into me. It was a painless procedure, and it took only a few minutes. All I had to do was strap the person down beneath the glass bell, activate the plunger, wait beneath the other glass bell, and the machine would do the rest. I can still remember how excited I was the first time I saw the sparks shooting from the open eyes of one of my factory workers, sailing through the clear rubber hose, and falling over me like rain. There's no better feeling in the world.

"The eyes, they say, are the windows to the soul. All I did, children, was find a way to shut those windows.

"It wasn't that hard. After all, I had hundreds of factory workers to experiment with. Of course without the lights in their eyes they became little better than robots, but every great invention has its price.

"Now I have more respect than I ever dreamed of. People fear me and admire me. They do what I want them to, and they don't even know why. All because of the sparks in my shadow. Most people never even notice the sparks are there, but they can't help but be affected by them.

"I have to admit, your friend Ned Hajimura caused me a certain amount of trouble. You see, he discovered what I was doing before I was ready for him. He was too big to fit inside the glass bell I had manufactured; obviously, though, I couldn't just let him go. He might have told the police about my machine, and the police have made it quite clear to me that they can't be trusted. Stealing my rhinestone jacket—the nerve! 'Sometimes things vanish from the evidence locker,' they said. But my rhinestone jacket didn't *vanish* from anything! It was taken! *Taken*, I tell you!"

Howard Thigpen's face was as red as a tomato by this time, and he had to take a few deep breaths to calm himself down. The sparks in his shadow were dancing about wildly. After his color had returned to normal, he continued, "So, I forced Ned Hajimura to stay here at the factory where I could keep an eye on him. It was really the only solution. After all, I had to put together a larger glass bell before I could fit him inside, and a thing like that takes time. Yesterday the new bell was finally ready, and I was able to remove the sparks from his eyes. I was finished with him in a matter of minutes. Unfortunately, he was my very last factory worker. Now I will have to move on to someone else.

"That's why it's so lucky that you kids came along when you did," he finished, sizing us up with his eyes. "The larger bell should fit the three of you rather nicely."

Ned Hajimura had been standing in the corner of the room all this time. His arms were hanging loose at his sides, and his face was following Howard Thigpen back and forth. There was no sign of the jitteriness we had noticed in him a couple of days ago. He could have been just another piece of office furniture, a fan or a plant or something.

It was true that Ned Hajimura had been kind of an oddball, but I had liked him anyway. It was sad to think that he was just like all the other factory workers now.

Howard Thigpen had just turned his back to us and was getting ready to leave the room when Emily Holmes spoke up. "We're not afraid of you," she said. "You can't take the light from our eyes."

He seemed amused by this. "And why ever not?" he asked, screwing his head around.

"Because our parents and teachers would notice," she said. "They would figure out something was wrong, and they would come after you."

I had seen Howard Thigpen smile before, but this was the first time I had ever heard him laugh. It sounded like a door creaking open on one of those haunted house CDs you always hear at Halloween. "The only thing your parents and teachers would notice is that you ate your vegetables without complaining and you turned your homework in on time," he said. "They would be delighted by the change. No, I can transplant your sparks any time I want to. But it will have to wait a little while," he announced. "Right now I have some business to attend to.

"I'll see you soon, children," he said. And with those words, he took Ned Hajimura and left.

A few seconds after he shut the door, Emily Holmes called out, "Rhinestone jackets look ridiculous!" but he didn't come back, so he must not have heard her.

NINETEEN

Howard Thigpen had made a point of locking the door behind him, and no matter how much we banged on it or jiggled the knob, we couldn't get it to open. There were no windows in Room 423, or any other obvious ways out, but we knew we had to keep looking. We couldn't let Howard Thigpen steal the light from our eyes.

The door was the kind that could lock from either the inside or the outside. We decided to conduct a thorough search of the room to see if we could find an extra key. Kevin Applebab rummaged through all the drawers in the desk and then through the stuff on top—the paper tray and the Rolodex and the pen-and-pencil organizer. Emily Holmes checked the lamp and the floor plant and the carpet art hanging on the walls. And I went through the filing cabinet, opening each individual file folder and looking for the glint of a metal key. None of us had the slightest bit of luck. Kevin Applebab found a roll of Scotch tape and a bag of airline peanuts inside the desk, but that was about it.

There's a character in *The Uncanny X-Men* named Kitty Pryde. Actually she's called Shadowcat now—they changed her name for some reason—but that doesn't matter. What's important is that she has this mutant power that allows her to make herself immaterial, which means that she can become as weightless as a ghost and pass right through things, floors and walls and ceilings and such. I know that it sounds kind of girly, but part of me couldn't help but wish that I was Kitty Pryde at that moment. I would have settled for any of the X-Men, but Kitty Pryde was the first one that sprang to mind.

Eventually, Emily Holmes and Kevin Applebab and I gave up on our search for the key. We didn't know what else to do. We sank down onto the carpet and waited for Howard Thigpen to come back. I'm not sure how long we sat there in silence like that. The factory bell went off a couple of times, so it must have been at least an hour. Even though we were all trapped in Room 423, it was hard for me to hear that bell without thinking, *Okay, time for our next class*, and reaching for my schoolbooks.

After some time had passed, Kevin Applebab asked, "What are you going to miss most about your life when you're a zombie robot?"

I had been thinking about exactly this, and I said, "I'm going to miss watching the fireflies come out in the fall. And reading all the new comic books each month. And eating Dim Sum and Then Some with my grandpa. What about you?"

"I'm going to miss going to Wild River Country in the summer," Kevin Applebab said. Wild River Country was North Mellwood's best water park, and Kevin Applebab was right—I couldn't even picture any of the factory workers wearing a swimsuit, much less shooting through a water chute or bobbing up and down in the wave pool. "What are you going to miss, Emily?" Kevin asked.

"I'm going to miss pretty much everything," Emily Holmes said, "but mostly I'm going to miss being able to see my sister, Cinnamon, when she comes home to visit. I haven't seen her in almost six months now."

For the next few minutes, nobody said a word. I didn't know about Kevin Applebab and Emily Holmes, but I was totally depressed. Not only that, I was starving. It had been at least half a day since I had eaten anything, and I could feel my stomach rumbling. Unfortunately, the only food in the room was the bag of airline peanuts Kevin Applebab had found inside the desk, and I couldn't eat those, on account of my rotten peanut experience.

Emily Holmes and Kevin Applebab shared the peanuts between them as I watched. There had been a box of miniature powdered doughnuts on my grandfather's kitchen counter that morning, and I wished that I had thought to bring them along with me. I was so hungry that I would have settled for a bagel even.

I still had my backpack with me, and I unzipped it to look for any stray potato chips I might have left there. I found my blue jeans, the Victrola horn, some notebook paper, a protractor, a stick with the bark peeled off, and a few pencils and pens, but no potato chips.

I took out the Victrola horn and the blue jeans and ran the needle along one of the grooves to see

heard, said, *Try the third ceiling panel from the door.* The second half said, *There's a tunnel there.*

The voice that came from my finger was small and still, but surprisingly easy to hear.

It wasn't mine. I didn't know *whose* it was.

Kevin Applebab and Emily Holmes were still gaping at me as though I had pulled a chicken out of my pants. "Stop it," I told them. "I don't know how it got there any more than you do."

"Do you think—?" Kevin Applebab began. He paused. "Do you think your finger is telling the truth?"

"How should I know?" I said. To be honest, the whole thing had me kind of weirded out.

"There's only one way to find out," Emily Holmes said as she stood up. She wheeled the office chair from behind the desk to the other side of the room. "One, two, three," she counted. "The third ceiling panel from the door." Then she stopped and climbed onto the chair. She poked at one of the ceiling panels. It was made of some sort of yellow foam with a rubbery white covering on the bottom. It shifted out of the way easily. "Hey, you guys!" Emily Holmes said. "Come take a look at this."

Kevin Applebab and I joined her beneath the ceiling panel. There were metal pipes and wooden beams to the right and left of the frame, but the space directly above it was hollow. When we stood on the chair and peeked our heads through, we could see a long crawlspace stretching in a straight line over the door.

"Holy cow!" Kevin Applebab said. "Your finger *was* telling the truth!"

"So what do you think?" Emily Holmes asked. "Should we try to get out this way?"

"I don't think we have any other choice," I said. "Who knows when Howard Thigpen will come back for us?"

I've never been very good at pull-ups, and the ceiling was a little too high for me to just lift myself through, even with the help of the chair. Kevin Applebab was tall enough that he could have hoisted himself up there without much trouble, but Emily Holmes had the same problem I did. In the end, the three of us decided to haul the desk across the floor, place the chair on top, and work our way up like we were playing on a jungle gym. One by one, we climbed inside the ceiling.

TWENTY

All of the ceiling panels were made of the same rubbery yellow foam as the first one. They were pretty flimsy, and we had to put our weight on the metal bars in between to keep from collapsing through. I crawled behind Emily Holmes, and Kevin Applebab crawled behind me. We tried to move as quickly as we could. We knew that as soon as Howard Thigpen unlocked Room 423, he would see that we had shifted the desk and chair to the middle of the room and figure out exactly where we had gone.

The tunnel in the ceiling was fairly dark, but there were cracks around the edges of the panels where the light shone through from below. The empty squares of light reminded me of the spaces on a chessboard. Everything sounded really loud to me—my backpack scratching against the roof, my blue jeans brushing against the bars of the ceiling, even my breathing. There were metal pipes and slanting wooden beams all around which kept us from crawling too far to either side. We kept pushing forward until I bumped into Emily Holmes, and Kevin Applebab bumped into me.

"What's the problem?" I asked Emily. "Why did you stop?"

"We're out of space," she said. We had run into a thick metal pipe that rose up through the ceiling like a tree trunk. "It's warm to the touch," she said. "Probably a steam pipe from one of the machines in the factory. There's no way around it."

"I bet we've gone far enough already," Kevin Applebab said. "Let's lift up one of the ceiling panels and see where we are."

I slid my panel out of the way and peered through the crack.

We had crossed over the hall and were directly above Room 422. I could see the Spark Transplantation Machine standing in the middle of the room. The glass bells on either side were curved at the top, which made the images beneath them stretch and warp into strange, balloonlike shapes. That's why it took me a minute to realize there was someone sitting inside one of them—the larger one. Whoever it was had been shackled to the chair and was struggling to yank himself free. I tried to make out his face, but I couldn't do it. I was getting ready to call out to him when Howard Thigpen walked into view. He stopped in front of the metal box that would activate the Spark Transplantation Machine, gleefully cracked his knuckles, and reached for the plunger. I slipped the ceiling panel back in place.

My heart was thumping like crazy. "It's Room 422!" I whispered to Emily Holmes and Kevin Applebab. "Howard Thigpen is there! I think he's about to transplant somebody's sparks. What should we do?"

"Was Ned Hajimura there?" Kevin Applebab asked.

"I didn't see him."

"Well," Kevin Applebab said after a pause. "Maybe your finger has another idea."

"Yeah," Emily Holmes agreed. "Check your finger."

I shrugged my shoulders. "If you think it will work . . ."

It was kind of hard for me to take the Victrola horn out of my backpack while I was crouched over inside the ceiling, but I managed to do it without losing my balance, crashing through the panel, and landing on top of Howard Thigpen, which is what I was afraid would happen. I tested my left index finger again. It contained exactly the same message that it had before: *Try the third ceiling panel from the door. There's a tunnel there.* In the closed space of the ceiling, the voice that came from my finger had a bit of an echo to it, but it wasn't so loud that Howard Thigpen would be able to hear it.

"Nope," I said. "Nothing has changed."

"Check the next finger then," Emily Holmes suggested.

I moved on to my middle finger. At first, all I heard was the same sort of static I had heard on the wallpaper of my bedroom, that dull skritching sound that reminded me of Kevin Applebab's hamsters. But then I found a message that was brand-new. *Open the hatch behind the plunger,* it said.

This was getting ridiculous.

"Is that all it says?" Emily Holmes asked. "'Open the hatch behind the plunger'?"

"That's it for this finger," I said. "Everything else is just skritches."

"What about the next one?"

The message on my ring finger was slightly longer than the messages on my index and middle fingers: *Plug the red wire into the green hole*, it said, *and the green wire into the red hole*.

"And the one after that?" Emily Holmes asked.

Disconnect the transplantation hose, my pinkie finger said.

I was more baffled now than ever. Not only were there announcements hidden in the grooves of each of my fingers, but the announcements appeared to be instructions for breaking the Spark Transplantation Machine. Where could they have come from, I wondered? The mystery was getting crazier every minute. I doubted even Sherlock Holmes could have solved it.

"So let's put it all together," Emily Holmes said. "What we need to do is (middle finger) look for a hatch behind the plunger on the Spark Transplantation Machine and open it, (ring finger) find the green wire and the red wire and switch their places, and (pinkie finger) pull out the hose that runs between the glass bells."

"That's about the size of it," Kevin Applebab said.

"But how do we know we can trust my fingers?" I asked.

"They haven't lied to us yet," Kevin Applebab pointed out. "They were right about the ceiling panel. Besides, we trusted the blue jeans and the potato chips, and that worked out okay."

This seemed like a convincing argument to me.

We decided that because we were directly above Room 422, we would each choose a ceiling panel to slide out of the way. Then we would jump to the floor at exactly the same time. Emily Holmes and Kevin Applebab would find a way to subdue Howard Thigpen, and I would take care of the hatch and the wires and the transplantation hose. Meanwhile, we would all keep a lookout for Ned Hajimura.

"Are you ready?" I asked.

Kevin Applebab and Emily Holmes nodded.

"One, two, three," I said. We pried our ceiling

panels loose and dropped to the floor. The fall was farther than I expected it to be. I landed crookedly, scraping my knee on the corner of a filing cabinet, but I didn't have time to think about it.

Howard Thigpen, it turned out, had already activated the plunger and was sitting inside the smaller glass bell. He looked up as soon as we came banging to the floor. He reached for the door to the bell, but Emily Holmes and Kevin Applebab were there in a flash. They leaned against it with all their weight. The door wouldn't budge.

"How did you kids get out of Room 423?!" Howard Thigpen yelled. "Guards! Help!"

But nobody came.

The man in the other glass bell had stopped jerking around. His chin had fallen onto his chest, and he was gazing into his lap like it was the most fascinating thing he had ever seen. At first, I didn't know what this meant: whether the light from his eyes had already been stolen or whether he had just tired himself out. Then I spotted the sparks swimming like tadpoles through the clear rubber hose between the bells—a dozen tiny prickles of light. I figured that the spark transplantation process was about halfway finished. In any case, it was easy for me to see who the man inside the other bell was from this angle. With his bushy gray beard and his silver badge, he could only be Earl the security guard.

Howard Thigpen continued to shout at Emily Holmes and Kevin Applebab as I looked for the hatch on the back side of the plunger.

"Let me out!" he said, and "I order you to lie down on the carpet!" and "I'll give you fifty—no, a *hundred* dollars—to release the door!" He beat on the walls of the bell with his fists. I could tell that it was hard for Emily Holmes and Kevin Applebab to ignore his commands—the lights in his shadow gave him an unusual hypnotic power—but they managed to fight him off.

The hatch behind the plunger was the kind with a half-moon-shaped ridge at the bottom to help you pull it open. "Found it!" I shouted, and I raised it on its hinges.

There must have been twenty wires inside— gray wires, blue wires, brown wires, you name it. But there was only one green wire and only one red one.

"Pretend you're spinning a hula hoop!" Howard Thigpen demanded. "Cluck like a chicken!"

Once, when I was a little kid, I jammed a fork I was playing with into a light socket. It didn't electrocute me or anything, but it did make an angry popping noise and spread a cloud of black soot over my arm. I was worried the same thing would happen when I tried to switch the green wire and the red one. Instead, though, the wires slipped smoothly out of their holes and smoothly into the new ones.

My fingers really *had* known what they were talking about.

The Spark Transplantation Machine, which had been humming loudly and buzzing softly, stopped dead when I took the wires out. Then, when I plugged them back in, it started up again. Only now it was *buzzing* loudly and *humming* softly. It took me a minute to realize what had happened: the machine had reversed directions.

The lights inside the clear rubber hose had stalled and were starting to travel the other way. Instead of transplanting the sparks from Earl the security guard to Howard Thigpen, the machine was going to transplant the sparks from Howard Thigpen to Earl the security guard.

By this time Howard Thigpen was just ranting. "Dance like an elf!" he shouted. "Swallow a lightbulb! Pretend you're Norwegian!" He must have figured out what I had done when he heard the machine switching off and powering back up again.

I grabbed for the transplantation hose, but even when I rose onto my tiptoes, it was a little too high for me to reach. "I don't think I can get it!" I told Emily Holmes and Kevin Applebab.

Kevin Applebab said, "I bet I can," and with barely a thought, he hooked his arm around the top of the glass bell, took the hose in his hand, and gave it a good yank. It popped right out.

"There are advantages to being six feet, two inches tall," he said.

Now the hose was dangling from the top of the smaller glass bell. Inside, Howard Thigpen was snatching at the sparks that were pouring out of his body. Thousands upon thousands of them were casting off like tiny boats and rising into the air.

"Candy bars! Toothbrushes! Blue jeans!" he was shouting. The sparks streamed out of the open end of the hose into Room 422. "Shaving cream! Pigpens! Potato chips! Tennis shoes!"

It was several minutes before the final spark came loose from his shadow and floated away. Howard Thigpen gave the door of the glass bell one last smack with his palms.

"Respect me!" he said, and then he whispered it. "Respect me."

He collapsed to the floor.

TWENTY-ONE

Because the transplantation hose had been disconnected from the other glass bell, the sparks had nowhere to go. They drifted around the room for a while, and then, all at once, they swarmed together and fell over the three of us in a shimmering rain. It was almost as if they had taken a vote. I could feel them zipping around over my skin and my clothing. They made me tingle from head to toe. It felt pretty good until I remembered that they were the lights from somebody else's eyes. I didn't particularly want to be the person responsible for a factory full of zombies, and I figured I had to find a way to get rid of the sparks.

Howard Thigpen was sitting with his legs stretched out in front of him inside the glass bell. He was staring straight ahead, looking at nothing at all. He was just like the factory workers we had been seeing all week. When Kevin Applebab and

Emily Holmes snapped their fingers at him, he barely moved. There was no need for them to hold the door shut any longer, so they let it go.

"How do we get rid of these sparks?" I asked. I was trying to shake them off by whipping my arms and legs around, but it wasn't working.

"I wish we could keep them," Kevin Applebab said. "They feel wonderful."

"I know. We can't, though. They're not ours."

"Well, the first thing we should do is turn the machine off," Emily Holmes said. "After that, I just don't know." She tugged on the plunger, and it lifted slowly out of the metal box. The Spark Transplantation Machine fell silent.

We decided that even if we couldn't do anything else, we could at least release Earl the security guard. He was in no better shape than Howard Thigpen, but if we set him free, we might be able to find a way to return the sparks to his eyes. We opened the door of the large glass bell, and I stepped inside, followed by Emily Holmes and Kevin Applebab.

As soon as Kevin Applebab came within a few inches of Earl the security guard, a strange thing happened. A dozen of the sparks that had been swimming over his skin leaped the gap between the two of them and landed on Earl. We could see them traveling up his arms, burrowing through the gray nest of his beard, and twisting past his cheeks and nose. Finally, they disappeared into his eyes.

Earl blinked a few times. He was wide awake. "Clarence, my amigo!" he said when he saw me. "What are you doing here? And why am I in these shackles?"

"It's a long story," I said to him. "I'll tell you later."

We found the key to Earl the security guard's shackles inside a small magnetic STOR-A-KEY box attached to the bottom of his chair. We unlocked him. We thought about tying Howard Thigpen up with rope before we left, or shackling him to the same chair that Earl had been in, but we were afraid that if we got too close to him, the same thing would happen that had happened with Earl: the sparks would jump from one or another of us, and he would wake up. We decided it was best just to leave him where he was, at least for now.

The four of us—me, Kevin Applebab, Emily

Holmes, and Earl the security guard—went down the long, twisting hall to the shaving cream factory. The machines were still making a racket as they pumped out globs of blue-green goo, and the factory workers were still standing in their places by the conveyor belt, gazing blankly ahead of them as the bottles drifted past.

When we got to the bottom of the stairs, Earl said, "I'd better find out who's manning the security booth. Things fall to pieces when I'm not around. I'll see you kids later." He left through the front door.

We were about to follow him outside when one of the factory workers brushed past us. A burst of sparks came loose from Emily Holmes, landed on the factory worker's neck and shoulders, and zeroed in on his eyes. As soon as they sank inside, he gasped and blinked a few times, touching his face.

He looked amazed to be alive. "I wonder what my wife is making for dinner tonight," he said.

I could tell that he wasn't really talking to us. He was just listening to the sound of his own voice.

It didn't take long for us to figure out what was

going on. The sparks from the Transplantation Machine had indeed attached themselves to us, but only loosely. Whenever we came across the person they actually belonged to, they would break free of our shadows and find their way home. We spent the next few hours walking through the seven factories, stopping by every factory worker we could find to return the light to his eyes. Occasionally one of the sparks would snag in place on our skin or our clothing, like a button with a loop of thread caught in its hole, and we would have to shake it loose. But for the most part, we got rid of the sparks without too much trouble.

One of the last people we saw that day was Ned Hajimura. He was standing by his bed on the top floor of the tennis shoe factory, staring emptily at his pillow. I put my hand on his shoulder. Right away, what must have been twenty or thirty sparks jumped from my shadow into his eyes—more sparks than I had seen with any of the other factory workers.

Ned Hajimura took a deep breath and gave a sudden yelp, the same noise he had made when we frightened him in the potato chip storage room. He was himself again.

When he saw the three of us he said, "Kids! Howard Thigpen! He's waiting for you! It's a trap!"

"We know," Emily Holmes told him. "It's all over."

"It's over?" he asked.

"Mostly," I said. "We put a stop to Howard Thigpen, and we shut down the Spark Transplantation Machine, and we've been giving the rest of the factory workers their sparks back all afternoon. But there's one thing I still don't understand. How did you record those messages in my fingerprints?"

"Fingerprints?" Ned Hajimura asked. "What messages in your fingerprints?"

I explained to Ned Hajimura how the voice that came from my fingers had given us step-by-step instructions on how to escape from Room 423 and reverse the Spark Transplantation Machine. I even played the instructions for him with my Victrola horn. He seemed really impressed.

"That's fascinating," he said. "But I had nothing to do with it. The only messages I recorded were

in the potato chips and the blue jeans. I wonder—"
he began, and he ran his fingers over his lips.
"Hey!" he exclaimed. "What happened to my
mustache?"

That was one mystery I couldn't solve.

We still didn't know what we were going to do
about Howard Thigpen. I mean, we couldn't just
leave him in Room 422 forever. But Ned Hajimura
told us not to worry about it.

"I'll take care of him," he said. "You kids have
done enough work for one day."

He said good-bye to us at the front door of the
tennis shoe factory, and we watched him shuffle
away.

As we were making our way across the courtyard, the factory bell rang again. Before we knew
it, we were wading through a mob of factory workers. Some of them were chatting with one another,
and some were stretching and yawning in the cool
spring air. Others were just looking around at the
sun that was shining off the puddles and the birds
that were curving through the sky toward
Mellwood Reservoir. Every so often, we would
brush past a factory worker whose sparks had not

been returned to him yet. We would wait there beside him as the light settled into his eyes, and then we'd watch him shake his head and slowly realize where he was.

By the time we left, there were still a few sparks left in our shadows, but not nearly as many as there had been before. It would be another month or two before we stopped bumping into different factory workers on the street and seeing clusters of sparks pop from our bodies like miniature fireworks and make their way back to the people they belonged to. Some of the sparks we would keep for years.

TWENTY-TWO

We took the Factory Row bus back across North Mellwood and got off at the bagel restaurant. It was dark by the time I made it home to the antique store. My grandfather was upstairs reading a magazine in his easy chair. He looked up as I walked past his door.

"I thought you were going to stay the night with that broomstick friend of yours?" he said. "What's his name? Kevin Yabbablab?"

"Kevin Applebab," I said. "I hurt my knee, so I decided to come home."

This was true. My knee was red and raw where I had scraped it against the filing cabinet in Room 422. It had already started to scab over, and I could tell that I was going to have a hard time working my jeans past the sore—not to mention past the bruises I had gotten during the pig battering incident.

"Is there anything to eat?" I said. "I'm starving."

"I ordered meatball sandwiches from Subs 'n' Such." He burped. "There are plenty of leftovers. They're in the refrigerator."

"Thanks, Grandpa."

"Don't thank me," he said. "Thank my dyspepsia."

The meatball sandwiches made by Subs 'n' Such are extraordinarily large, almost the size of a dinner plate, as well as extraordinarily sloppy. Subs 'n' Such is known for them, not only in North Mellwood but throughout the Greater Mellwood area. The one in the refrigerator was more than enough to fill me up. I ate it with a bag of pretzels and a can of grape soda.

I finished dinner just in time to watch my third-favorite television show, *The Famous TV Robot Variety Hour*. *The Famous TV Robot Variety Hour* comes on every Saturday at eight o'clock and stars a bunch of robots from old science fiction shows—*Lost in Space*, *Small Wonder*, and *Buck Rogers in the 25th Century*— along with a different guest robot every week. The robots do juggling acts and comedy sketches and song-and-dance numbers. At the end of every episode they wave good-bye to the camera while the orchestra plays a song called "Mr. Roboto." The audience always sings along with this song: *"Thank you very much-o, Mr. Roboto."* There's nothing else like it on television.

At the end of *The Famous TV Robot Variety Hour*, a news bulletin came on. "We have some breaking news for you at this hour: Howard Thigpen, founder and CEO of the Thigpen Corporation, has been hospitalized at the North Mellwood Psychiatric Institute after suffering an apparent mental breakdown. Doctors at the institute say that Thigpen is in stable physical condition, but displays extreme lack of feeling. He is slow to respond to questions and does not appear to recognize the sound of his name. The institute plans to hold him for further observation. Channel thirty-eight will bring you more on this story as it develops."

I put some ointment and a Band-Aid on my scraped knee and spent an hour or so reading comic books before I finally went to bed. I slept like a baby.

TWENTY-THREE

You might think there wouldn't be too much for me to do around my house on Sundays, but it's actually the busiest day of the week for me. Every Sunday, I help out my grandfather in the store in exchange for my allowance. I don't know what it is about antique shoppers and Sunday afternoons, but it's obviously something. The bell on the door-knob just won't stop ringing.

That particular Sunday, I stood behind the cash register collecting money and making change. Occasionally I helped one of the customers load a floor lamp or a wicker table into the car. I didn't have time to do much of anything else. Before I went downstairs for the day, though, I did do one thing—I checked the fingers on my right hand for messages.

In the factory I had only tested the fingers on my left hand, and it had been bothering me ever since. I am right-handed, so it was even harder for me to control the Victrola horn using my left hand than it had been the day before using my right. After a few tries, though, I was able to do it.

What I heard wasn't exactly the rustling sound that meant there was nothing recorded inside my fingerprints at all, but it wasn't exactly words either. It sounded like somebody mumbling something very quietly. No matter how carefully I listened, though, I couldn't quite make out what that somebody was saying. Maybe the voice would get louder as I grew older and my fingers got bigger. The more I thought about it, the more I hoped so. I was expecting a growth spurt at any time.

Shimerman was already working at the front counter when I got downstairs. He knows all sorts of unusual things about the human body—from why men have nipples to what causes hiccups—and I knew that he would be the perfect person to ask my question to. "Hey, Shimerman," I said. "Where do fingerprints come from?"

He scratched at his stomach through his gray-pink recycled-lint shirt. "Where do fingerprints come from? People are born with them."

"Yeah," I said, "but how do they get there in the first place?"

"Well, they're created while you're in the womb. They show up around the age of five months. See, there are about ten million cells per square centimeter of skin. That's a lot of cells. Even identical twins have different fingerprints."

That wasn't much help. "What I really want to know, I guess, is who puts them there?" I said.

It was the sort of question most people would just answer with a shrug, but not Shimerman.

"That's an interesting question, Young Ruggles. But there's no one answer," he said. "Some people would say that genetics puts them there. Some people would say it's just a matter of chance—the cells happen to come together in a certain way, and that's all there is to it. And some people would say that it's God."

"What would *you* say?" I asked.

"I would say that anything is possible," he said. "Maybe someday we'll know for sure, but probably not. Some mysteries just can't be solved. Oh! And speaking of questions without answers—" He lifted a stack of "Ghostbusters" records from the floor and placed them smack on top of the counter. "Do you know anything about these? We found them behind that tepee of broken water skis yesterday, and neither of us knew where they came from."

"They're mine," I told him. "I'm keeping them for a friend."

"Well, that's one mystery solved, at least." Shimerman nodded. "Your grandfather wanted me to throw them away, but I convinced him to let me hold onto them. Do you need any help carrying them upstairs?"

Before I could answer, a knot of customers came through the door.

"Shimerman!" my grandfather yelled. "Get back to work! Stop corrupting my grandson!"

We left the "Ghostbusters" records on the floor behind the front counter.

The rest of the day passed in a blur. Before I knew it I had eaten lunch and dinner and my after-dinner snack, and I was asleep and dreaming in my bed.

The next morning was a beautiful one. I walked the three blocks to school with the sun and the wind on my face, just watching the leaves shiver on the trees. The kids in the courtyard let me pass without whispering or staring at me. They had lost interest in me over the weekend. Apparently, one of the ninth graders had been flicking Flamin' Hot Cheetos at the monkeys in the Mellwood Zoo on Saturday when one of the monkeys had gotten mad and thrown a handful of his you-know-what at him. That was all anybody wanted to talk about.

It wasn't until the five-minute warning bell rang and I took my seat in Mr. Fred's class that I realized I had forgotten something.

"Did you write your proposal yet?" I heard one of the girls who sat behind me saying.

"Of course," said another girl. "I'm going to test which type of music makes plants grow faster—country, classical, or heavy metal."

"I'm going to do mine on optical illusions."

"'Which Animal Is Smarter—Cats or Dogs?'" somebody else said.

"'Which Hamburger Restaurant Has the Most Bacteria—McDonald's, Wendy's, or Burger King?'"

"'How Much Food Coloring Does It Take to

Color an Entire Swimming Pool?'"

With all the excitement at the factories, my science fair project had completely slipped my mind. I knew that Mr. Fred would be disappointed in me, particularly after he had shared his pizza with me and given me the "Ghostbusters" records and everything.

When the second bell went off, Mr. Fred stood up from his desk and began taking roll. I noticed him tapping his fingers on the podium as he read off our names: "Todd Brown. Leah Carlisle. Katie Cooper. Devin Corbin."

Everything seemed to be happening very quickly. I was watching Mr. Fred's fingers move up and down when I had my brainstorm. I knew what I would do for my science fair project! Maybe Shimerman was right, and there were some mysteries that couldn't be solved. But science wasn't only about solving mysteries—it was also about exploring them.

I tore a sheet of paper from one of my notebooks, scribbled my name at the top, and wrote a description of my idea as quickly as I could.

"Okay, folks," Mr. Fred said when he had

finished taking roll. "We've got a lot of work to do today, but before we get started I want you to pass your science fair proposals to the front of the room. Hurry up now. Chop, chop."

I finished writing just in time to hand my proposal to the kid sitting in front of me. "Victrola Horns and Hidden Messages," it was called. "A New Way to Tell If Your Fingerprints Really Are Unique."

Acknowledgments

I owe thanks to my editor, Katherine Tegen, my agent, Jennifer Carlson, and to Noah Walker, Pam Strickland, Meg Rains, and Heather McDonough for early readings, as well as to Emily Holmes— the real one—for the generous loan of her name.

Kevin Brockmeier is the author of CITY OF NAMES and several novels for adults, including THE BRIEF HISTORY OF THE DEAD. He has published stories in *The Georgia Review*, *The New Yorker*, and *McSweeney's*. He is also the recipient of many prestigious honors, including a James Michener–Paul Engle Fellowship, the *Chicago Tribune*'s Nelson Algren Award, and three O. Henry Awards. He lives in Little Rock, Arkansas.